A large swell lifted me up. For a moment I was higher than Michi, and I could see what he was pointing at. Roughly fifty feet to my left, a patch of water fizzed and rippled as a shoal of tiny minnows leapt into the air.

Suddenly, I found a hidden reserve of energy. The splashes made by the leaping fish were nothing compared to mine. Arms swinging like windmills, I went churning away from the unseen menace that swept towards me beneath the terrified minnows.

But I wasn't fast enough ...

## EXTREME ADVENTURES

**BOOK 3**

# SHARK BAIT

## JUSTIN D'ATH

**Kane Miller**
A DIVISION OF EDC PUBLISHING

First American Edition 2010
Kane Miller, A Division of EDC Publishing
Revised cover, 2012

First published in 2006 by Penguin Group (Australia)
Text copyright © Justin D'Ath 2006

Library of Congress Control Number: 2009943488

Printed and bound in the United States of America
2 3 4 5 6 7 8 9 10
ISBN: 978-1-61067-119-4

*For Mitsumasa Aoki*

# RUN!

No other fish on the Great Barrier Reef is quite as cute, or as harmless, as the tiny orange and white clownfish. Yet I blame a clownfish for what happened. One made famous around the world, thanks to a movie.

"Nemo!"

I looked around in surprise. The Japanese boy was waving at me. Up until that point, we had mostly ignored each other. We'd both been too busy exploring the narrow shelf of reef exposed by the low tide. Besides, there was the problem of communicating.

"Nemo!" he called again, and pointed down into a shimmering tide pool.

I made my way towards him, skirting a colorful coral garden and being very careful where I placed my good foot.  The reef might be a "natural wonderland," like all the tourist brochures say, but a whole range of dangers lie in wait for the unwary: stonefish, stingrays, fire coral, blue-ringed octopuses and deadly sea wasps, just to name a few. But little did I suspect, as I wobbled up to the Japanese boy crouching on the coral shelf at the very tip of the island, that the greatest threat to our safety that afternoon had nothing to do with the reef. It would come from the sparkling aquamarine expanse of the Coral Sea behind us.

The Japanese boy was wearing yellow inflatable water wings over his T-shirt. It wasn't a good look, but who was I to judge? I had one foot encased in plaster, with a huge black trash bag taped around it, and split tennis balls jammed onto the ends of my crutches to help me walk on the reef.

"What have you found?" I asked, laying my modified crutches on the coral beside me as I crouched to look.

He removed his wraparound sunglasses and pointed into the water. At the bottom of the pool, partially obscured by a semicircle of yellow plate coral, a pair of clownfish nestled among the fleshy tentacles of a large mauve sea anemone.

"Nemo," he repeated.

He knew no English; I knew no Japanese. But we had both seen the movie.

"Nemo," I said, returning his smile.

The sea breeze ruffled the boy's short, spiky hair. Without his sunglasses, he reminded me of someone, but I couldn't think who. He only looked about ten or eleven, much younger than me. But that didn't matter; it would be good to have someone to hang out with besides the twins. My family had been at the resort for nearly a week, and we were all growing a bit tired of each other's company. The Japanese boy and his parents had the cabin next to ours. We were neighbors, but the language barrier had kept us from introducing ourselves. Until now.

I tapped my chest. "I'm Sam."

He gave a little bow. "*Oai dekite ureshii desu*, Sam," he said shyly. Then he touched his own chest. "*Watashi no namae wa* Michi *desu*."

It sounded complicated. "So you're called … Michidesu?"

"Michi," he corrected me.

"Glad to meet you, Michi," I said.

He bowed again, and for a moment, Michi and I smiled at each other. Then, because there was nothing else we could say, we turned our attention back to the fish. They were cute all right, and very much like the ones in the movie. But soon I would wish we had never laid eyes on them. If we hadn't been so preoccupied with the two Nemo look-alikes, we might have noticed the danger before it was too late.

Michi saw it first. Suddenly, he gripped my arm and yelled something in Japanese. I reached for my crutches and struggled upright. *Holy guacamole!* I couldn't believe my eyes. Something weird was going on. The horizon had changed – it looked higher than it had a minute ago. And *much* closer!

Michi started talking flat out in his own language. Most of it meant nothing to me, but one word snagged in my brain: *tsunami*.

Then I said an English word – *Run!* – and Michi didn't need a translation for that either.

# FISH FOOD

You can't run on a coral reef. Especially if you're on crutches. There are slimy ridges, unexpected holes and big, fragile sea fans that break away beneath your soggy sneaker. There are gorgonian whips that wrap themselves around your crutches, razor-sharp staghorn corals that graze your shins, and spiny black sea urchins that sting your hands when you fall over. You spend half your time on your hands and knees. Or up to your waist in water. Wading, wallowing, staggering, falling, and who cares about the threat of stonefish, or the fact that you've dropped your crutches.

Michi wasn't doing much better than me. He was

wearing a pair of brown leather shoes with smooth soles, and he kept sliding all over the place. Somehow he stayed on his feet, but he wasn't going much faster than I was.

We both could have saved our energy. It was obvious from the start that we weren't going to make it. The long finger of exposed reef extended five hundred feet out to sea. Michi and I were at the end of it when we first saw the wave. But it's impossible *not* to run when you turn around and there's half the Coral Sea steamrolling towards you in a ten-foot-high wall.

Michi was wrong: It wasn't a tsunami. It was just a freak wave, that one in a million when the currents, the tides and the winds all combine to produce a monster.

Umpteen mega gallons of seawater came crashing over the reef in a frothy white boil that picked Michi and me up and tossed us like matchsticks into the sea on the other side.

I don't have much memory of what happened next. I recall a swirl of bubbles and sandy green water, bits of broken-off coral and twisting strands of seaweed and a couple of dislodged starfish turning pinwheels above me.

*Were* they above me? It was impossible to know what was up and what was down. My hands clawed for the surface, but *where was the surface?* I seemed to be doing cartwheels or somersaults, or perhaps both. It was strangely quiet. After the thunderous roar of the wave smashing across the reef, now there was an almost eerie absence of noise. I found myself in a silent green world. It felt like a dream – a dream that was rapidly turning into a nightmare. My lungs were caving in!

Then, the nightmare was over. A sudden flash of sunlight made rainbows in my eyelashes, telling me not only that I was awake, but that my head was above water. I took a series of huge, gulping breaths, greedily filling my lungs with oxygen. There was water up my nose, and I felt a bit shaken, but otherwise I seemed to be okay. I just needed to get to shore.

But where *was* shore?

A passing wave lifted me up, and I glimpsed a line of miniature coconut palms poking over the horizon about a mile away. My heart nearly stopped beating. How could I have come so far? Then it dawned on me. *Good one, Sam, you're facing the wrong direction!* I was looking at Cowrie Island, the small, uninhabited neighbor of the popular resort island where we were staying.

Treading water – not so easy with a plaster cast on one foot – I turned a clumsy semicircle in the pitching green sea, and breathed a big sigh of relief when I saw a strip of white sand framed by palm trees – *the right size* palm trees this time – no more than two hundred feet away. Utopia Island, right where it was supposed to be.

But it appeared to be *moving*!

*Wrong again, Sam.* The island wasn't moving, *I* was. A strong current was carrying me along parallel to the beach. If I didn't get to shore quickly, it would push me past our island and out into the open sea. I loosened my single sneaker and kicked it away. Mum and Dad were going to kill me – first I lose my crutches, now I'd lost my shoe – but the plaster cast on my other foot was a big enough handicap on its own. Besides, my parents could hardly blame me for the freak wave that had washed Michi and me off the reef.

Where was he, anyway?

"Michi?" I called, anxiously looking right and left as another wave lifted me up.

There was nothing around me but empty sea.

The waves were coming around the reef and moving through the strait between the two islands. As each one bore me up, I searched frantically for Michi. There was no sign of him. I yelled his name at the top of my voice, but the only reply was the screech of a lone sea eagle circling high overhead. I was becoming seriously worried now. Michi had been wearing water wings, but what if they'd ripped on the sharp corals? Or – worse still – what if they'd caught on an underwater snag, preventing Michi from regaining the surface?

I kept searching for another two or three minutes. I must have called Michi's name a hundred times, but there was no response.

*He isn't dead*, I thought. He *can't* be dead!

"Michiiiiiiiiiiiiiiiiiiiiiiii!" I yelled, with the last of my breath.

I was puffing now and struggling to stay afloat. I didn't know how much longer I could last. My left foot, with its big lump of plaster, was growing heavier by the moment. Water was getting in, seeping under the plastic. It felt like a bag of wet cement was strapped to my leg. Soon it would drag me down. *Too bad about Michi*, I thought. I had to save myself.

I was about to turn for shore when I saw a speck of yellow at the top of a distant wave. It was there one moment, then it disappeared behind another swell. But that single glimpse was enough. Along with the flash of yellow water wing, I had seen a waving arm.

Michi was alive!

He was about two hundred yards from me – two hundred yards further out to sea. I treaded water, hesitating. To my right, the beach was drifting steadily past. Each wave pushed me another yard or two further away from the deserted shore. In a few more minutes, I would be clear of the island.

Would I be able to swim back against the current with a great lump of waterlogged plaster on my foot?

Not likely. I would wind up feeding the fishes.

Then I thought of Michi. How he'd bowed at me when he'd introduced himself. How he'd pointed out the clownfish and proudly said, "Nemo."

Wishing that neither of us had seen the movie, I turned my back on Utopia Island and struck out into open water.

# "BOOSS!"

The current helped me – it pushed me along.
But it did the opposite for Michi. Although he was
trying to swim back in my direction, the water wings
restricted his arm movements, and he wasn't making
any progress against the strong current. He seemed
to be going backwards. I struggled after him, doing
a kind of splashy dog paddle with my body hanging
nearly vertical in the water because of the weight on
my left foot. If I didn't reach Michi soon, the saturated
plaster cast was going to pull me down. Some
rescuer! Now *I* was the one who needed rescuing. I
hoped Michi's water wings were buoyant enough to
keep us both afloat.

But first I had to reach him. I was going forwards; he was going backwards. It was a life or death race. I was gaining on him, but my progress was getting slower and slower as I ran out of energy and my plaster cast took on more water.

Finally, just a hundred feet short of Michi, I had to call it quits. I was exhausted. I could not swim another stroke. My plaster cast must have weighed twenty pounds. It was a struggle just to keep my head above water. I shot a panicked glance back in the direction of Utopia Island. Only the treetops were visible over the heaving green sea. I would never get back there now.

I was going to drown!

*Don't panic*, I cautioned myself. I had been in worse predicaments than this and had gotten out of them. The number one rule in a tight situation is to remain calm.

But it's hard to remain calm when all your energy is focused on keeping your head above water, and then someone starts yelling at you in a language you don't understand.

"Booss! Booss! Booss!"

I gasped at Michi, "Don't … understand …

Japanese."

He had lost his sunglasses, and his eyes were round with fear. "Booss! Booss!" he screamed, pointing to my left.

Just my face was above water. I couldn't see anything in the direction he was pointing. And I didn't want to waste my energy talking, especially when neither of us could understand the other. Whatever *booss* was, it would have to wait until I reached Michi.

*If I reached him*, said a realistic part of my mind.

A large swell lifted me up, and for a moment, I was higher than Michi. Suddenly, I could see what he was pointing at. Roughly fifty feet to my left, a patch of water fizzed and rippled as a shoal of tiny minnows leapt into the air.

*Big deal*, I thought. *Here I am drowning, who cares about a few jumping fish?*

"Booss! Booss! Booss!" screamed Michi.

What was the matter with him? Couldn't he see I was nearly drowning? Then something clicked in my brain.

Not booss, *Bruce*!

I watched the patch of broken water come rippling towards me. My whole body turned to jelly.

Now I understood what was going on. The minnows were jumping because they were trying to get away from something below the surface. Bruce. It was the name of another character in the Nemo movie – the great white shark.

Suddenly, I found a hidden reserve of energy. The splashes made by the leaping fish were nothing compared to mine. Arms swinging like windmills, I went churning away from the unseen menace that swept towards me beneath the terrified minnows.

But I wasn't fast enough.

*Thump!*

It felt like a rugby tackle, only without the accompanying clinch of hands and arms. Just a bone-jarring impact against my hip. I felt myself knocked head over heels. The next moment I was upside down, looking back through the inverted V of my splayed white legs. The seawater made my vision fuzzy, but I had a pretty good view of the shark. It was swimming away from me, its brown, streamlined body weaving from side to side as it disappeared into the murky green distance. Hit and run. I completed my terrifying somersault and clawed my way back to the surface, spitting out a big mouthful of seawater, my eyes stinging.

"*Daijoubu desu ka*, Sam?" Michi called, splashing his way towards me.

I guessed he wanted to know if I was okay. I was wondering the same thing myself. Gingerly, I reached down and touched my hip. It felt a bit bruised, but my shorts weren't even ripped.

"I'm okay, Michi," I gasped.

I couldn't believe that a real live shark had just head-butted me and then swum away. I couldn't believe it hadn't taken a chunk out of me. I couldn't believe how lucky I was to be alive.

That was a big shark!

I was in shock, trembling like a leaf, and so distracted by what had just happened that I forgot about the plaster cast on my foot.

Until the weight of it dragged me under.

Suddenly, I was back in the blurry green undersea world. And the shark was there too. Coming straight at me. Fast!

# KILLING MACHINE

Here's something I didn't know about sharks: When they attack something that's too big to fit in their mouth, sometimes they head-butt their victim first. To stun it.

Then they come back to feed.

Here's something the shark didn't know about me: I wasn't stunned. I could fight back.

But it wasn't an even match. This was a thirteen-foot tiger shark, a thirteen-hundred-pound killing machine armed with enough razor-sharp teeth to take out a fully grown tuna with one bite. I was a one-hundred-thirty-five-pound boy, armed with nothing more than a deep fear of becoming shark food. But survival is a strong instinct. When the shark came rushing in for the kill, I aimed a karate kick at its nose.

On dry land I'm an orange belt, but that doesn't count for much under the sea. Underwater, a human is very much out of his natural element, whereas a shark is right at home. Rolling effortlessly onto its side, the giant fish opened its bear-trap jaws, and my foot went straight in.

*Crunch!*

That bite should have killed me. At the very least, it should have taken my foot off at the ankle. But the only pain I felt was a sharp twinge in my knee as my leg doubled back on itself. The next thing I knew, I was being dragged through the water. My foot was locked in the shark's jaws while the rest of me trailed alongside its brown, sandpapery body like a human pilot fish. But pilot fish go forwards, not backwards. And they don't hurt sharks. I grabbed hold of a big pectoral fin and gave it a sharp twist, sending the shark into a series of crazy barrel rolls. On one of the rolls we broke the water's silvery surface, but before I had time to breathe I was underwater again, back in a world of green, surrounded by bubbles, spinning. There was no feeling in my foot. Perhaps the nerves had been severed. There wasn't time to think. Finally, the shark stopped spinning and began shaking me in its mouth, like a dog playing with a kid's stuffed toy. Because we were underwater, our movements were slowed down, otherwise I might have been shaken to death. I had lost my grip on the fin and dangled by one leg just below the shark's head. Its big silver-and-black eye looked down at me. The saltwater made everything blurry, but I was close enough to see a snarl of hooked, bristling teeth chewing on my foot.

I was about to die, yet I felt strangely calm. Shock does that to you. It's the mind's natural anesthetic when all hope of survival is gone, and you know your time's up. But that doesn't mean I was *happy* about it.

*You ugly, overgrown anchovy!* I thought, and gave the shark a power strike.

Okay, it wasn't much of a hit – karate was never intended to be used underwater – but the edge of my hand hit my attacker in the eye. It probably surprised the shark more than hurt it, but as my karate instructor says, "Surprise beats size." Distracted by the unexpected blow, the shark lost its grip on my foot. Suddenly, I was free. But not out of danger. The huge brown fish circled slowly, as if it was thinking about having a second try at me. Finally, it must have decided that there were easier meals to be had in the sea – and more digestible ones. It spat out a big lump of plaster, then went zigzagging silently away.

# SHARK BAIT

I should be grateful to that shark. It saved my life. If it hadn't come along when it did and tried to eat me, I would have drowned for sure. Luckily, the shark bit down on my plaster cast in the corner of its mouth, where the teeth were relatively small and widely spaced, so it couldn't close its jaw the whole way. It only managed to crack the plaster. When it released me, part of my cast remained in its jaws like the broken half of a walnut shell. The other half was still taped to my leg. All I had to do was rip off the shredded trash bag. Then I was free to kick my way to the surface.

Michi grabbed me under the arms and supported

me while I recovered. *"Watashi wa anata ga same ni yarareta to omonoimasita!"* he said.

But I couldn't talk in any language, even my own. I was too busy gasping and spluttering and coughing up water. I must have swallowed half the Coral Sea during my battle with the tiger shark.

Finally, I got my breath back. Holding onto Michi's water wings to keep myself afloat, I ducked my head back under the sea and looked around in every direction. There was no sign of the shark. But I saw something else that surprised me. Michi was still wearing his brown leather shoes. No wonder he'd been having so much trouble swimming!

I was about to surface again and tell him to get rid of them, when I noticed something. There was a reddish-brown stain in the water. I came up for air, then ducked my head straight back down. It was blood! All around us, the water was stained with blood. Where was it coming from? I looked at my foot – I looked at *both* my feet – then I looked at my legs and my arms, but I couldn't see any cuts or injuries. If the blood wasn't mine, then it must have been Michi's.

I gulped more air and ducked my head back

under. Sure enough, there was a long, jagged gash on one of Michi's legs.

"Did Bruce do that?" I asked, gasping for breath.

At the mention of Bruce, Michi looked set to jump right out of the sea, like one of the minnows we'd seen earlier. I quickly shook my head, to reassure him that the shark hadn't come back.

"You're hurt," I said, pointing down.

Michi's eyes bugged out. He hadn't been aware he was injured. It must have happened when the monster wave hit – a piece of sharp coral must have sliced Michi's leg open. That explained the shark attack. Normally sharks leave humans alone, but blood in the water will make them aggressive. The tiger shark must have been attracted by the smell of blood and mistaken me for its source.

Which was lucky for Michi. And lucky for me too, as things turned out.

But now the blood was a problem. Not only because Michi was losing it, but because of what it might attract. A bleeding wound in the open sea is like an invitation to every marine predator and scavenger for miles around, telling them there's a feast on. If we didn't stop the blood in a hurry, Michi and I were shark bait.

There was still a strip of tape stuck to my leg where I'd ripped away the remnants of the trash bag. I peeled it off and held it up to show Michi. Then I pointed at his leg. He nodded in understanding and helped me position it over the long, bleeding gash on his calf. The tape was no longer very sticky, but it stopped most of the blood. As long as it stayed in place, we would probably be okay. Now our only problem was getting back to the island. It was a big problem. The island was about half a mile away. Most of the time we couldn't even see it. It only rose into view when we floated over the largest swells. And each swell carried us a little further out to sea. Or *in* to sea, I suppose, because the current was pushing us back towards the Australian mainland.

"Take your shoes off," I said to Michi. "We'll try to swim back to the island."

He gave me a blank look.

"Shoes," I repeated, pointing down. I mimed undoing shoelaces, but Michi shook his head.

"Bruce," he said.

I tried to explain that shoes would be no help at all if another shark attacked, but I couldn't get the message across. Michi kept shaking his head.

23

He was determined to keep his shoes on, so I gave up arguing. Part of me knew it would make little difference whether Michi kept his shoes on or not. The island was too far away, and the current was too strong. We would have to wait to be rescued. Our families would have noticed we were missing by now. They would send boats looking for us. There were several powerful speedboats at the resort. It would only take ten minutes to reach us. I hoped with all my heart they would find us before nightfall.

At least there was no longer any danger of drowning. I clung to Michi's water wings and wriggled my toes in the water. My foot felt okay. A big old rodeo bull had stomped on it six weeks earlier. The doctor planned to remove the cast when we got back from our holiday, but Bruce the tiger shark had saved him the trouble.

Thoughts of the attack sent a rash of goose bumps tingling across my skin. *Don't think about sharks*, I told myself. But it was hard not to, surrounded by all that sea, our legs dangling in the water in full view of whatever might be down there.

"Bruce," whispered Michi, as if he could read my thoughts.

I was about to say, *don't even joke about it,* when the words died in my throat.

Because Michi wasn't joking.

# NO MERCY

There seemed to be about four of them, although it was difficult to be sure. Seldom was more than one fin visible at a time. The darting gray triangles broke the surface for just a second or two, then disappeared. They were circling us, never coming closer than about twenty or twenty-five yards, but that was still too close for comfort.

I couldn't see what kind of sharks they were. They looked smaller than the tiger shark that had attacked me earlier, no more than seven or eight feet long. Reef sharks, I hoped, because they're not supposed to be dangerous. But whatever kind they were, the circling sharks were obviously interested in us. They must have smelled Michi's blood. The strip of tape was still in place, but its edges looked bubbled and loose. I got Michi to scrunch his knees up against his chest and put both hands over the tape to keep it in place. It would have been easier without the weight of his sodden leather shoes, but now I kind of envied him for having something on his feet.

I pulled my own legs up too. That's supposed to be the best defense against shark attack. My brother Nathan is a tour guide with an adventure company in the Northern Territory, and he told me about it once. Don't dangle your feet, and if there's more than one of you, bunch together so you won't be mistaken for a fish or a seal. But holding your legs up, even underwater, even when you've got a pair of inflated water wings to hold on to, is pretty tiring if you have to do it for a long time. My muscles started quivering. The sharks had been circling for about an hour, and it was growing dark. Where was the rescue boat?

At one point we heard the faraway burble of an engine. Both of us started yelling as loud as we could – me in English, Michi in Japanese – but as soon as we stopped, our voices thin and scratchy from shouting, the only sound left was the splash and lick of the sea.

And the occasional swirl of a shark's fin breaking the surface.

The sun had gone down. As daylight faded, the sharks grew bolder. A dark triangle zipped past, no more than thirty feet away. Another went sliding by in the opposite direction. Then a third fin broke the surface a few yards beyond the other two. Just its tip was visible. It carved a wide semicircle through the black water, turning slowly in our direction. Then, suddenly, it accelerated.

Michi gasped, and his skinny fingers dug into me as the shark came straight at us, its fin going down as it approached until all we could see was a long, V-shaped ripple coming towards us like an arrow. We pulled our feet up and tensed ourselves. I wished I could jump out of the sea like a minnow. I felt a flurry in the water just beneath the soles of my feet, but no head-butt, no crunch of teeth, no white explosion of pain.

One after another, all the sharks began these mock attacks. They would come darting towards us flat out, then veer away at the very last moment. They seemed to be building up courage, egging each other on. If one got bold enough to actually snap at us, that would be it – there'd be a feeding frenzy.

Michi and I held on to each other, teeth chattering (though not from cold), legs scrunched up beneath us, totally helpless. We were completely at the sharks' mercy. And mercy, to a shark, is an unknown concept.

Night falls fast in the tropics. Within two or three minutes, we could see nothing but a wide scatter of stars in the sky and their dancing reflections on the water around us. With the onset of night, a stillness had settled over the sea. It had become calm. And completely silent. Where were the sharks? I could no longer hear the swirl and hiss of their fins. All I could hear was Michi's shallow breathing and the racing thump of my pulse in my ears.

*Splosh!*

In the light of the rising moon, I saw the dark silhouette of a fin rise out of the water less than three feet away. It was so close I could have touched it. But no way was I going to touch it. I pulled my legs up until my knees nearly bumped my chin. The big, curved fin rolled back into the water, glistening in the moonlight as it disappeared.

*Slurp!*

Another fin appeared on the other side of us, then

another, and another after that. They were all around us. There must have been ten of them, and none was further away than about twenty feet. The night was filled with their splishing and splashing and slurping.

Then – *shishkebab!* – one actually brushed against me. When I felt its long, slippery body go sliding past my arm, I jerked away so violently that I bumped heads with Michi.

"Okay! Sam, okay!" he said breathlessly.

Okay? How could I be okay? We were surrounded by sharks!

Michi gripped both my shoulders. I could just make out a big, goofy grin on his face. "Not Bruce," he said.

Was he blind? Was he deaf? I held my breath as a tall black fin slid past my ear.

"There's a whole pack of Bruces!" I gasped.

Michi shook his head. He was still smiling. I couldn't believe it. How could he be smiling at a time like this?

Releasing my shoulder, Michi pointed at a long black shape that curled out of the water ten feet to our right. *"Sokoni iruka ga iru."*

"I don't understand Japanese," I whispered.

Then one of the sharks made a loud *whuffing* sound. As if it was … breathing.

*Hang on, sharks don't breathe*, I told myself. And suddenly, I realized what Michi was trying to tell me. These weren't sharks.

"Not Bruce," I said, nodding excitedly. "Dolphins!"

# TOP 40

The dolphins must have chased the sharks away. They seemed quite friendly, but perhaps it was just curiosity causing them to mill around us. Apart from the one that had brushed against me in the beginning, they wouldn't let us touch them. They stayed with us for another four or five minutes, then swam off into the night.

It was sad to see them go. Sad and scary. I'd felt safe in their company (once I knew what they were!), and I reckon Michi had felt the same. Now we were on our own again. In the middle of the Coral Sea. In the dark.

I spent the next half hour stressing about the

sharks. Where were they? Would they come back? But as time passed, I began to feel more confident that they were gone for good. It was fully dark now. The sharks wouldn't be able to see us. They had probably gone back down to the reef, or wherever they'd come from.

"The Bruces have gone," I said to Michi.

He didn't understand me. I could feel him shivering, even though the tropical seawater felt as warm as a bath.

"No Bruces," I said slowly.

"No Bruce," Michi repeated, his voice small and scared.

"Michi and Sam okay."

"Michi, Sam, okay," he whispered bravely.

Poor kid, I thought. He only looked about ten, and he probably came from a big city where the scariest thing that could happen would be the power going off. His school shoes suggested he wasn't the outdoors type. So did the water wings. What self-respecting ten-year-old would wear water wings?

A *live* one, I thought. One I owed my life to. If it wasn't for Michi's water wings, both of us would have drowned hours ago.

I wished we could communicate better. "Are you from Tokyo?" I asked, pronouncing each word slowly.

He shook his head. "Nagoya," he said. Then he pointed to me. "*Anata wa* Sydney *kara kita no desu ka*?"

I guessed he was asking if I was from Sydney. "Crocodile Bridge," I told him.

Michi's eyes grew big in the moonlight. "Crocodile!" he whispered. Obviously that was a word he understood. But it wasn't a good subject to think about when you're floating in the middle of the Coral Sea at night. Saltwater crocodiles *do* sometimes visit the reef. And during a cyclone last summer, I'd tangled with enough saltwater crocodiles to last me a lifetime.

"Crocodile *Bridge*. It's a town near Darwin," I explained.

"Ah, Darwin," Michi nodded.

He knew more about my country than I knew about his. Where was Nagoya? Was it a city or a town? The language barrier was so frustrating. If only we'd been able to talk, we might have distracted each other from scary thoughts of saltwater crocodiles and sharks, and whether or not we would ever be rescued. Talking would have helped pass the time too.

According to my watch, which was waterproof and had a light-up dial, it was only 9:30 p.m. We were swept off the reef at about five, so we'd been in the water for four and a half hours. It seemed like we'd been there forever. Daylight was still nine hours away. *Nine more hours!*

I glanced up at the sky, which was filled with tiny, blinking stars. It gave me an idea. Clearing my throat, I began – hesitantly – to sing.

> *"Twinkle, twinkle, little star,*
> *How I wonder what you are ..."*

I sang it all the way through to the end, feeling embarrassed and silly. I'm probably the world's worst singer. I'd been hoping Michi might sing along with me in his own language. I thought for sure there'd be a Japanese version of "Twinkle, Twinkle, Little Star."

I heard Michi clear his throat. Then he began singing. It wasn't a nursery rhyme, but it was a song I knew – Kelly Clarkson's latest single. And he was singing in English! At the start of the second verse, I joined in. Or tried to. I couldn't hit the high notes like Michi could, and I stumbled in some places where I'd forgotten the words, but Michi led me through. He knew the song better than I did.

It turned out that Michi could sing nearly every song in the Top 40, and lots more besides. They must have a radio station in Nagoya that plays overseas hits, and Michi must listen to it all the time.

We sang for half the night. Michi was an unreal singer. He could hit all these impossibly high notes, like a choirboy on TV. Compared to him, I sounded shocking. My voice was breaking, and it kept switching from low and raspy one moment, to high and squeaky the next. But I didn't care. There was nobody to hear us and complain, and singing kept our minds off being lost at sea. It also helped us to forget how scared and hungry and thirsty we were.

Most important of all, it kept us awake. I was worried about drifting off to sleep. Our survival depended on staying awake and alert throughout the night.

But we couldn't go on singing forever. By two in the morning, after going through all the songs we knew about fifty times, it became increasingly hard to concentrate. I found myself repeating the same lines over and over. Sometimes I switched from one song to another without realizing it. Michi lapsed into Japanese. His voice grew quieter and quieter. Finally, he fell silent, and his head tipped slowly sideways until it rested on one of the pale, squashy water wings. He was asleep. I didn't wake him. The water wings would keep him afloat.

Unlike Michi, I had to stay awake. *It was important to stay awake*, I told myself. Very important. But I was so tired that I could no longer remember why. *Don't go to sleep*, I kept telling myself, fighting to keep my droopy eyelids open. *Don't go to sleep. Don't ... go ... to ...*

I must have dozed off finally, otherwise I would have heard the boat before it got so close. Suddenly, it was right there. Its white bow wave came churning out of the darkness like an avalanche.

*Holy guacamole!* It was going to plow straight into us!

# INDESTRUCTIBLE

You don't think in a situation like that – there isn't time. You simply act. I brought my knees up between Michi and me, placed both feet squarely against his stomach, then pushed with all my might.

Although it was dark, there was just enough moonlight to see Michi's eyes snap open in shock as he came awake, and the black "O" of his mouth as he screamed, then the boat's enormous bow came slicing directly between us.

I dragged my legs out of the way, but not quickly enough. The boat struck me a massive blow on the thigh. It spun me around, rolling me helplessly along the hull beneath the water line. My eyes were open, but it was too dark to see anything but a pale mist of bubbles swirling around me. The hull made a dull thump every time I hit it. I heard the surge of water and the rumble of engines. There was another sound too, a heavy *thwop, thwop, thwop* that grew steadily louder.

The propellers! I had to avoid them, or I'd be chopped to ribbons!

The hull whacked me again, on the shoulder this time. I felt it roll across my back. I counted the seconds – one, two, three – then I pushed with every ounce of energy I could summon from my tired arms and legs. My timing was perfect. Both hands and both feet made contact with the hull at the same time. All four pushed together. I spun out into the black water. The churning wash from one of the propellers parted my hair – that's how close I came to having my skull split open – but the deadly blades missed me. I was okay.

I bobbed to the surface seven or eight yards behind the boat. It was a big, ocean-going launch. There were no lights anywhere on board, but I saw a man's silhouette on the flying bridge. The lower deck was stacked with what looked like crayfish pots. Three burbling outboard motors glinted in the moonlight as the powerful launch sped away from me.

"Hey!" I yelled, waving my arms frantically. "Stop! Help us!"

The lone figure at the helm turned and looked back in my direction, but the boat continued on its course. Its engine-note didn't change. *He can't have seen me*, I realized, still shaking from the shock of nearly being run down. He must have mistaken my yelling for the cries of a seabird. I stopped waving and shouting and turned my attention to the dark water around me.

"Michi?"

"*Kochira desu!*"

A dark shape came splashing in my direction. I heaved a big sigh of relief. I had tried to push Michi out of the boat's way, but I hadn't been sure if I'd succeeded. I swam to meet him.

It was only when we reached each other that I noticed something had changed. Michi was hanging lower in the water. Only one of his water wings supported him. The other one, though still attached to his shoulder, was shredded. It must have been chopped by the boat's propellers.

"Michi, are you okay?" I gasped, terrified that the propellers had chopped him as well.

"Okay," he said, then held up his arm to show me he wasn't injured.

I gave him a high-five. Michi and I had experienced some pretty rough moments over the past ten or twelve hours, but we had handled everything the reef could dish out, and we'd survived.

"We're indestructible!" I yelled, at the wide, starry sky.

It took about ten seconds for the reality of our situation to bring me back down to earth. Or down to *water*, I should say – and that was the problem. We were still lost and adrift in the middle of the Coral Sea, with no chance of being rescued until daylight.

Why hadn't that launch stopped? The man on the flying bridge had turned around and looked back. He seemed to look right at me. Okay, maybe he mistook my shouts for a seabird, but surely he would have seen me waving. I had seen *him*, after all. The starlight was quite bright. And why wasn't his launch showing any lights? I didn't know much about boats, but I was ninety percent sure that it was illegal to go out to sea at night without turning on the lights on your boat.

I was *one hundred* percent sure that it was illegal to see someone in the water, waving and calling for help, then go cruising away, leaving them to drown.

But Michi and I were not going to drown. We were indestructible. Deep down, I knew this wasn't true, but I couldn't give up hope now. I looked at my watch and saw there were still three hours to go until dawn.

Those were the longest three hours of my life. Michi dozed off from time to time, but I stayed awake. I had to. Now that we had only one water wing, we weren't as buoyant as before. I tried floating on my back, but even then I had to kick my feet slowly to keep myself on the surface. It was very tiring. After a while I got into a rhythm and shut my mind to my aching calf muscles. I guess it was like running a marathon. You put your body on autopilot and occupy your brain with something else. I played counting games to distract myself.

I invented a game where I'd count slowly to one thousand, then do a countdown all the way back to one. When I got to one, I had to guess the time. Then I'd look at my watch to see how close I was. It probably sounds dumb, but it kept me occupied and awake. I became so absorbed, in fact, that I didn't even realize dawn was breaking until Michi interrupted me.

"Bruce."

"Ninety-eight, ninety-seven, ninety-six ..."

"Bruce," Michi repeated.

I was in a kind of trance and didn't really catch on to what he was saying. But he'd distracted me from my counting. Was I up to ninety-five, or nine hundred and five? I frowned at him, annoyed, and that was when I realized dawn was breaking. It wasn't fully light yet, but it was light enough to see two tiny islands on the horizon. We hadn't been swept away as far as I'd thought.

Then I noticed Michi's expression. He looked terrified. And sounded it too.

"Bruce!" he yelled.

It finally sank in. I snapped out of my trance and glanced over my shoulder in the direction of Michi's boggle-eyed gaze. And nearly had a full cardiac arrest.

Weaving towards us across the blue-green sea was a dorsal fin, roughly the size of a yacht's keel.

# HITCHHIKERS

The shark was so big it seemed wrong. Its head, a massive, wedge-shaped shadow in the green water, seemed as wide as a car. Its pectoral fins looked like the wings of a F18 jet fighter. And it was sweeping towards us, with the momentum of an express train. There was no time to get out of the way.

"Pull your feet up!" I screamed at Michi.

It made no difference that Michi didn't understand English. You can't watch a fifty-foot shark approach you at full speed without taking evasive action. We both pulled our feet up. I was scared half out of my mind, there's no denying it, but in the other half an idea was forming: *We were facing the oncoming shark and Utopia Island was directly behind us. That meant ...*

As the enormous, white-spotted head passed beneath us like the prow of a nuclear submarine, I wrapped one arm around Michi's skinny body.

*Here goes nothing!* I thought.

With my other hand, I grabbed the huge dorsal fin as it churned past.

Michi must have thought I was crazy. He closed his eyes and gritted his teeth as the monster shark began towing us through the waves. I fought to hold on. The fin felt like sandpaper, and I had a good grip, but the drag of our two bodies through the water nearly pulled my arm out of its socket. Changing my hold on Michi, I shouted at him to open his eyes, then swung him around to the other side of the shark's tall, triangular fin.

"Grab hold!" I gasped.

Michi looked dazed, like someone having a bad dream, but he gingerly took hold.

"B-B-Bruce?" he stammered, peering at me wide-eyed across the bulge of foam churned up by the massive shark's fin.

I shook my head. "Not Bruce," I said. "Whale shark."

I had seen them on TV. Whale sharks are the

world's largest fish. They grow to nearly sixty-five feet in length and can weigh as much as fifteen tons. But they're harmless. They feed on small fish and plankton. Because of their massive size, they aren't scared of humans. Sometimes they even let divers ride on their backs.

Michi and I weren't divers. We didn't ride the whale shark, we simply let it drag us along the surface. As long as its fin stayed above water, I reckoned we'd be okay. But if it dived, we'd have to let go in a hurry.

Luckily, the whale shark stayed near the surface. Maybe that's where the plankton were at that time of day, or perhaps the water was warmer there than down in the jungle-green depths below us. The oversized fish didn't seem to mind having two hitchhikers hanging onto its three-foot-high dorsal fin. After a few minutes, Michi grinned at me, and I grinned back. For the first time since we'd been swept off the reef, our luck seemed to be changing. If the whale shark remained on its present course, it would take us right past the larger of the two islands on the horizon.

# 10

# SPAGHETTI
# AND MEATBALLS

The shark didn't deviate. It was going to pass within a few hundred yards of Utopia Island. As we drew nearer, the long, low mound of trees and coconut palms seemed to rise out of the sea ahead of us. I longed for a glimpse of the resort, but it was on the other side. It didn't matter. Even if nobody spotted us when we let go of the shark, I reckoned we could to make it ashore on our own.

I no longer had the heavy plaster cast to hamper me, and I didn't think the current would be so strong at this end of the island.

"*Asoko wo miro!*" Michi cried suddenly.

I looked where he was pointing. The tiny figure of a

man stood on a sandy point halfway along the island. Although we were several hundred yards away – too far for our voices to carry – Michi and I both began shouting and waving our free arms above our heads.

We shouldn't have done it. Our carrying-on disturbed the whale shark. With a sudden swirl of water, and an unexpected downward tug of its dorsal fin, the huge fish was gone. Michi and I were left floundering in the waves.

We took a few moments to recover. Both of us had swallowed large mouthfuls of seawater when the shark dived. Spitting and coughing, I splashed over to Michi. Without the shark's fin to hold on to, we were floating lower in the water, and we could only see the man when we were lifted up by waves. He was turned sideways to us and held something up to his face. Binoculars. He seemed to be looking at the sky.

Michi started waving and shouting again, but I motioned him to be silent. I touched my ear, indicating that I wanted to listen. The sound was faint, but unmistakable. A big grin spread slowly across Michi's face when he recognized it. I smiled back. It was the buzz of an airplane.

A dot appeared above the horizon. The buzz

increased to a dull roar. As the aircraft sped towards us, I saw that it wasn't the little red-and-white seaplane that brought tourists to the island. This was much larger, with four engines. It was a big Navy Orion. There could be only one reason why an Orion would be flying out to Utopia Island so early in the morning. They were searching for Michi and me. We were saved!

Instead of coming in our direction, the Orion roared low across the pale dawn sky to our right. It seemed to be heading for Cowrie Island. Michi and I waved our arms madly, but it continued unerringly on its course.

*C'mon guys, you've got the wrong island!* I wanted to yell at them.

Michi touched my arm and pointed. In the excitement of seeing the search plane, I had forgotten about the man on the beach. He was no longer there. From the top of the next wave, I noticed something else. There was a small, narrow bay just beyond the sandy point where the man had been standing. Deep in the bay, partially hidden beneath some overhanging trees, was a big blue-and-gray launch.

"*Soko ni booto ga arimasu!*" Michi said excitedly.

I nodded to show that I had seen it too. But the boat was too far away, and anyway, the man hadn't seen us. We would have to make it to shore on our own. I mimed a paddling motion in the direction of the beach.

"Swim," I said.

Michi nodded. "*Oyogimashou!*"

We didn't get far. Less than halfway to shore, something wrapped around my ankle. It was cold and leathery. *Seaweed*, I thought. I stopped swimming and tried to kick it away, but the seaweed clung to me. Worse, another cold tendril curled around my other leg. Now I had seaweed around both legs. This was getting serious. I tried pulling my feet up, but the seaweed came with them. Because I wasn't paying attention to the sea, a wave took me by surprise. It washed over my head, and for two seconds I was in a blurry, underwater world filled with wriggling green seaweed. I bobbed back to the surface.

*Wriggling?* I thought.

"*Hebi da,*" Michi whispered.

I was nose-to-nose with him. He had stopped swimming too. He wasn't looking at me. His eyes were swiveled down, watching a green rope of seaweed that was draped diagonally across his shoulder. It seemed to be moving, threading itself slowly through the narrow gap between the water wing and his neck.

As the seaweed moved, Michi slowly tipped his head to one side, away from it. I heard him take in a long, shuddering breath, like someone trying to control their emotions. Then I felt a cold, feather-light touch on the back of my own neck, just above the water line. It sent a chill through my whole body. This wasn't seaweed, I realized, not daring to move as a small, evil-looking head poked out of the water right beneath my nose. It flickered its Y-shaped tongue at me.

Sea snakes. They were all around us. All over us. One came sliding up onto my shoulder, had a close look at my mouth (clamped tightly shut), then made a sagging bridge across the gap between Michi and me. It passed another one coming the other way. Now there was a snake looped around my neck. And one slithering across my head! I could feel them underwater, nosing at my limbs, tangling in my clothes, tickling past my feet. For thirty feet in every direction, the sea writhed and churned like a saucepan full of boiling spaghetti, with Michi and me in the middle of it.

"Stay absolutely still," I whispered to Michi.

He couldn't understand what I was saying. In fact, I don't think he even heard me. He seemed to be in shock. His face had turned a sickly bluish-gray, and just the whites of his eyes showed between half-closed eyelids. Every so often, a big tear would roll down one of his cheeks.

"Michi, it's going to be okay."

He gave his head a tiny shake. "*Hebi*," he whimpered, between chattering teeth.

There was nothing I could do to calm him. It was hard enough staying calm myself.

According to a program I saw on the Nature Channel, sea-snake venom is much deadlier than land-snake venom, but luckily, sea snakes aren't aggressive towards humans. They're just curious. They might swim right up to you to check you out, but they won't bite if you remain calm and don't do anything to alarm them. Good advice. In theory. But I wonder if the experts on the Nature Channel have ever been the human meatball in the snake spaghetti?

Here's another thing I heard on that program: Over the years, there have been a number of unconfirmed reports of sea snakes congregating in large, floating spaghetti-islands, like the one Michi and I got caught up in, but no scientist has ever seen it. If I were a scientist, I could be famous. But right now, I was more concerned with survival than scientific discovery. I just wanted to stay alive.

I don't know how long it lasted. When you're tied up in a floating tangle of several thousand deadly sea snakes, time passes slowly. All I could do was cling to Michi and try to keep him from freaking out totally.

I sang to him. I sang several of the songs we'd sung last night, but I kept forgetting the words. Finally, Michi's lips began moving. Almost silently at first, then louder, Michi joined in and sang with me. It seemed to help. He stopped shaking, his eyes opened, and some of the color slowly returned to his face.

Finally, after what seemed like hours – but was probably no more than fifteen minutes – we found ourselves at the edge of the writhing mass of snakes. They were lighter than us, and the surface current was carrying them slowly away. I waited until the last one had unwrapped itself from around my leg, then I carefully nudged Michi out into clear water.

"Let's get out of here," I whispered.

Michi let out a large breath. "*Wakarimashita!*" he replied, and the corners of his mouth twitched upwards in the ghost of a smile.

# WORSE THAN VERY BAD

After more than twelve hours at sea, it was wonderful to feel the first touch of solid land beneath my feet. Except it wasn't solid land, it was coral reef. And this time, my feet were bare. *It would be the very worst bad luck*, I thought, *to tread on a deadly stonefish now, only forty yards from the beach, after we'd been through so much and survived so many dangers*. I quickly lifted my feet off the coral and continued swimming.

"Don't put your feet down!" I called over my shoulder to Michi, a few strokes behind me. I kept forgetting he didn't understand English. Turning towards him, careful to keep my feet clear of the sharp coral three feet below, I pointed down into the cloudy green water and shook my head. "Coral reef," I said. "Very bad."

Michi pointed down too and said something in Japanese. I noticed he wasn't moving. His body was upright, his chest and shoulders clear of the waves. He was standing on the coral.

I shook my head and made the swimming motion. "Swim!" I urged him. "Reef, very bad."

Michi pointed down. "Very bad," he said.

He'd spoken English, but he was simply repeating something I had said. He still hadn't moved. Frustrated, eager to get to shore, I pointed impatiently towards the beach. "C'mon, Michi, we're almost there!"

He shook his head and spoke slowly, clearly. "Michi, very bad."

I hoped he didn't know what he was saying. But the expression on Michi's face was chillingly familiar. It was the look he'd had when he'd said, "Bruce." I searched the sea around us for sharks' fins. There weren't any, but I still felt nervous.

"Let's get out of the water, Michi," I said.

He still didn't move. "Very bad," he whispered.

What was wrong with him? Why wasn't he

coming? We could be on the beach in half a minute. I swam out, grabbed one of his wrists and gave it a small tug. "Come on, Michi, stop playing games!"

He didn't budge. He looked terrified. His eyes became moist, and his lower lip trembled as he pointed down at his feet. I couldn't see anything. The water was cloudy with sand stirred up by the passing waves. There was no blood, as far as I could see. But something was down there – something *very bad*, if Michi's English was accurate. Filling my lungs with air, I dived down to have a look.

*Shishkebab!* It was very bad, all right – *worse* than very bad. Michi wasn't following me ashore. He wasn't going anywhere – he wasn't able to.

I figured out what had happened. When I'd stopped a minute earlier and put my feet down, Michi must have done the same. But rather than touching coral, his feet went straight into the open maw of a giant clam. It had snapped closed around his ankles like a monstrous Venus flytrap. The huge shellfish was three feet wide and must have weighed four hundred pounds. There was no way that I could move it and no way to pry it open. I would have to go for help.

When I tried to explain this to Michi, he kept

shaking his head and clasping at my arms and wrists. He didn't want me to leave him.

"*Watashi wa okaasann to otoosann ga hituyou desu*," he said, tears in his eyes.

I didn't blame him for being scared. The sea level was halfway up his body, and some of the larger waves rose up almost as high as his neck. I wasn't sure whether the tide was coming in or going out. If it was coming in, Michi would be completely underwater in twenty minutes. There was no time to lose.

I showed him my watch. "When *that* gets to *there*," I said, pointing first at the minute hand, then at the three, "I'll come back and free you."

I don't know how much he understood, but Michi nodded and tried bravely to smile. Then he lifted one trembling hand out of the sea and gave me a high-five.

"In … de … struc … tible," he whispered.

I reached the shore in record time and struggled cautiously upright. I had been worried about my foot – the one that had been in plaster until just a few hours ago – but it seemed okay when I put weight on it. My legs weren't so good though – they felt weak and wobbly. Jelly legs. It was hard to balance.

The beach seemed to tip and sway beneath me. Until now, I hadn't realized how tired I was. How sleepy. When I tripped on a clump of vines, I lay still for several moments. The sand was so soft, so comfortable, so *dry*, and my body craved rest. *But I could rest later*, I told myself, scrambling back to my feet. Michi's life was in my hands.

I only looked back at him once. The sea *was* rising; I saw that right away. And the sight of Michi's lonely figure standing chest-deep in the waves was almost too awful to look at. He waved at me as I was about to enter the trees, and I waved back.

Part of me wondered if that was the last time I would see him alive.

# 12

# HOW CAN A RESORT DISAPPEAR?

It wasn't there! I had crossed the island, fighting my way through a jungle of trees and palms and tangled undergrowth, only to discover that the resort wasn't where it was supposed to be.

*Impossible!* I thought, running along the curved white beach in a panic. How can a tourist resort just disappear?

I came to a heavy thicket of mangroves standing on their roots like trees on legs. That was strange. The manager at our resort reckoned there were no mangroves on Utopia Island. I stopped running and turned around, narrowing my eyes because the orange rim of the sun had just appeared above the horizon.

*The sun shouldn't be over there*, I thought. It should rise in the east, not in the south.

Then the truth hit me. I wasn't *on* Utopia Island! The current that had swept Michi and me away from the island must have changed course during the night. Instead of continuing in a westerly direction, we had floated in a huge semicircle around the back of Cowrie Island and out to sea again, ending up far to the southeast. From that perspective, Cowrie Island would have appeared on the left of Utopia Island, instead of the other way around. And Utopia Island would have looked smaller because it was further away. The whale shark had brought us to Cowrie Island!

In the distance, the Navy Orion was still flying in wide, slow circles over the sea near Utopia Island. There was no doubt in my mind that they were looking for Michi and me, but they weren't going to find us over there. We were over here. *We* were the ones on the wrong island. And if I didn't think of something quickly, Michi was going to drown.

Suddenly, I remembered the man on the beach. He had a boat. He could save Michi! But he and his boat were halfway down the island and on the other side. I should have gone there first, instead of running around looking for a resort that didn't exist. Now it would take me at least fifteen minutes to reach him, then ten *more* minutes for the boat to reach Michi. I looked at my watch. Already fifteen minutes were gone. Michi had only six or seven minutes left!

I charged back across the island, crashing through the bushes and vines and dangling branches like a stampeding buffalo. When at last I came belting out of the trees, only Michi's head was visible, a tiny black dot in the wide turquoise sea. He saw me and cried out, waving both hands desperately above his head. I waved back and ran down the beach. What was I going to do?

My brother gave me some advice once about dealing with emergencies in the outdoors. He said to treat your surroundings as a friend, not an enemy. That way, Nathan reckons, you can make nature work *for* you, rather than against you.

I looked around for something that would work for me. What I needed was a strong stick to pry the clam open, so that Michi could get his feet out. There was driftwood all along the beach, but most of it was the wrong shape, or badly eroded by sea worms.

There were also some bits of trash – an old flip-flop, part of a styrofoam float from a fishing net, a red drinking straw. None of it was any use to me, so I ran back up to the edge of the forest.

I found a broken branch dangling from a tree. It looked exactly right for what I needed. I began wriggling it from side to side to break it free, but I was interrupted by a choking scream. When I turned around, Michi was gone! Suddenly, he reappeared, but only for a moment, then another wave rolled over him. Between the waves, which came every five or six seconds, Michi gulped desperate mouthfuls of air. He was drowning before my eyes!

I pulled and twisted at the branch. A strong sinew of white wood attached it to the tree. It would take another minute or two to break it off. Michi might drown in that time. I looked around helplessly for other broken or fallen branches. There weren't any. Michi screamed my name. I ran back down the beach. *Make your surroundings work for you*, Nathan had said. Scooping up the drinking straw, I ran into the sea and hurled myself headfirst into the waves.

When I reached him, only Michi's face was above water. His head was tipped all the way back so he could breathe. Every few seconds, he had to hold his breath and close his eyes as another glassy green wave swept over him. He gasped in surprise when I poked the straw into his mouth.

"Michi, breathe through it," I said, making blowing and sucking noises so he would understand.

He nodded and closed his lips firmly around the straw. Now he had a snorkel. It would keep him alive for a few more minutes. Enough time, I hoped, for me to return to shore, twist the branch off the tree and swim back with it.

As I set off for the beach once more, I was not at all confident that the branch would do any good. The giant clam was huge. To pry it open would take more than a branch. It would take an iron crowbar, or a stick of dynamite.

*Or a miracle*, I thought.

# 13

# ONE CHANCE IN A HUNDRED

I was only part of the way back to shore when something brushed across my belly in the gap between my T-shirt and shorts. Something cold and leathery. Something that gave me goose bumps all over.

I stopped swimming and carefully searched the sea around me. Bingo! About four yards to my right, a large patch of water roiled and churned with sea snakes. It must have been the same snake island that Michi and I had been caught up in earlier. This time, I didn't swim away from them, as any sensible person would have done. I was remembering my brother's advice: *Make your surroundings work for you.* And thinking: *What I'm about to do is totally crazy.* It had about a one percent chance of success. But if I didn't try it, Michi had a *one hundred* percent chance of drowning. Taking a deep breath to settle my jittery nerves, I kicked my feet up to the surface and swam straight towards the writhing spaghetti of deadly sea snakes.

Most of the three-and-a-half-foot-long reptiles were twisted together in a single, floating mass, but one or two swam free of the group like guards patrolling its perimeter. It must have been one of these guards that had brushed against my belly. Now another one came wriggling through the water to meet me. Who knows what its intentions were – perhaps it was merely curious – but I didn't wait to find out. As soon as the snake came within reach, I grabbed it behind the head. Or tried to. But in the rise and fall of the sea, I missed my mark and caught hold of it too far back.

The glistening olive-green sea snake twisted its head around and bit me.

Luckily, it struck my watch strap, otherwise I might have been dead within minutes. I didn't give the snake a second chance. Grabbing its neck with my other hand, I yanked it off my watch. This time I had a secure hold, just behind its small gray-green head. The snake went psycho. It coiled itself into a writhing green football around my wrist and arm, its mouth biting and snapping in my tightly clenched fingers. I treaded water, holding the angry creature well clear of the rest of me, and began backing cautiously away from the other snakes. But one of them had seen what was going on. It came threading through the water towards me like a wobbly, living arrow.

There was no mistaking this snake's intentions: It meant business. I swam backwards as fast as I could, but the reptile caught up with me in seconds. It darted past my kicking feet and swam up alongside my body. My head was above water, and I couldn't see the snake clearly, so I rolled over and ducked beneath the surface. The snake swam in a circle and came at me from behind. Spinning around, I used the arm holding the other sea snake to fend it off. The attacking snake came looping around it and lunged at me, missing my elbow by inches. It didn't slow down. With a quick flurry of its long, slightly flattened body, the reptile came sweeping under my arm and snapped its jaws closed on the trailing edge of my T-shirt. Before it could let go, I grabbed the second snake with my left hand, just behind the head, and pulled it free. Its fangs tore two long, jagged holes in the fabric.

Holding my two writhing captives clear of my body, I bobbed back to the surface. The other snakes were eight or nine yards away. I nervously searched the water between them and me. With a snake in each hand, I would be totally defenseless if another one attacked. There was no sign of any more guards. I began swimming backwards away from them, as fast as I could.

Only when I was far enough away from the snake island to feel safe, did I look out to sea. For a moment all I could see was water, and my heart skipped a beat. Then I saw a dark shadow beneath a glassy green wave. And above it, poking out of the water, was the tip of a red drinking straw.

I couldn't swim normally with a snake in each hand. I had to float on my back and kick myself along. It was slow going. Every passing wave pushed me back a foot or more. When I finally reached Michi, only about an inch of the straw cleared the surface. Waves rolled right over it. But after each wave had passed, a small fountain of water would shoot out of the straw, followed by a desperate suck of air.

Michi was completely underwater, but he was still breathing, still fighting to stay alive. It was a fight he couldn't win. The tip of the straw would be completely underwater in about a minute, and then …

It wasn't something I wanted to think about. Everything depended on the two snakes in my hands.

Michi's eyes were closed. He didn't know I was there. Both my hands were full, so I touched him with one foot to let him know I'd returned. His eyes snapped open, but he could barely look at me because his head was tipped so far back. That meant he couldn't see the snakes, which was probably a good thing. I nodded to him, as if to say, *I'll have you free in a moment*, then jackknifed my body and dived down to the coral bed at his feet.

My first attempt didn't work. I couldn't maneuver in the water because I had a writhing sea snake in each hand. The undertow swept me six feet from where I wanted to be. I surfaced and allowed the snakes to breathe, then tried again. This time I made allowance for the undertow and dived a couple of yards inshore from Michi. As I neared the coral bed, the current carried me towards him. I hoped.

There was a lot of stirred-up sand, and my eyes were stinging from the saltwater. I couldn't see where I was. Then a blurry shape drifted into view. A pair of blue shorts, two pale skinny legs, and the massive, rounded bulk of the giant clam.

I couldn't stop myself in the current, and my shoulder bumped into Michi's legs. I felt him struggling for balance, but I shut my mind to his panic. The huge, wavy jaws of the clam shell were passing directly beneath me. This was my one and only chance. Bringing both hands forward and down, I plunged the sea snakes headfirst into the clam, one on either side of Michi's trapped feet.

Then the current swept me and the snakes away.

Did it work? Did the snakes even bite the clam? I had no idea whether their venom would have any effect on the monster shellfish, nor how fast it would act if it did. I hoped it would stun the clam rather than kill it – stun it just enough to make it relax its grip on Michi. But the undertow had dragged me away before I could see what happened. Nor could I see anything else. I was surrounded by cloudy green water. My lungs were bursting. With a sea snake in each hand, I fought my way to the surface. Blinking seawater from my eyes, I looked back expectantly in Michi's direction. And saw nothing but empty water all the way to shore. It hadn't worked.

I had known all along it was a crazy idea, but even a one percent chance had been worth trying.

Fighting back tears, I carefully unwound the sea snake from my left wrist using the two free fingers of my right hand, then tossed it as far away from me as I could. I was about to unwind the second snake when a cloud of bubbles broke the surface three yards away. And Michi popped up!

He was still wearing his yellow water wing, and the red drinking straw was still in his mouth. He spat it out and coughed a few times. Then he turned in my direction and gave me a wet thumbs-up.

"Indestructible!" he gasped.

# HUNTED

I helped Michi to shore. He was shaking and very weak, and I had to half-carry him for the last thirty feet. We collapsed side by side on the beach.

"You're still wearing your shoes, you goof!" I laughed. But secretly I was annoyed. I'd spent half the night kicking my feet to help us stay afloat, and Michi's heavy leather shoes had made my job that much harder.

But I stopped being annoyed when Michi took off his shoes and socks, and I saw the livid purple bruises the clam's jaws had made on his heels and lower ankles. Without the protection of his shoes, who knows how bad his injuries might have been? The piece of tape I'd used as a makeshift bandage on his leg was gone, but the gash looked clean and was no longer bleeding.

"Can you walk?" I asked, and mimed a walking motion with my fingers.

I helped him to his feet. Michi let go of me and grinned. "Michi … walk … okay," he said softly. He took two shaky steps, then flopped forward in a dead faint.

He wouldn't wake up. It was a combination of exhaustion, lack of sleep and dehydration. I didn't feel very strong myself, and my eyelids were droopy, but Michi was small and light. I carried him past the high-tide mark to a grove of small coconut palms that would shade him from the rising sun. As I made Michi comfortable in the cool white sand, tucking the water wing under his head like a pillow, I got the strange feeling again that I knew him from somewhere. He looked so familiar. But there was no time to think about that now – I had to go for help.

It took me longer than I expected to reach the bay where I'd seen the launch. There were a lot of mangroves further along the beach, and getting through them was like negotiating an obstacle course.

Finally, they forced me away from the shore and into the lush forest that covered most of the island. It was hard going in my bare feet, but easier than crawling through the mangroves. I heaved a big sigh of relief when I finally heard voices through the trees ahead.

It sounded like two men. I couldn't hear what they were saying above all the squawking and chatter of birds. Up to that point I hadn't noticed many birds on the island, but I didn't give it more than a passing thought.

The men would get a big surprise to see me. In my head, I began rehearsing what I'd say. First, I'd ask for a humungous drink of water and maybe something to eat. Then, as we motored around in the launch to pick up Michi, I would tell them about my fight with the big tiger shark, and how some dolphins had saved us from the reef sharks, and about the whale shark that had pulled us to Cowrie Island. I couldn't wait to see the looks on their faces when I told them how I'd freed Michi from the giant clam with the help of two deadly sea snakes. I reckoned they would think I was a bit of hero.

It didn't turn out quite as I expected. In my prepared speech about Michi's and my adventures,

I forgot one very important detail: the big, ocean-going launch with no lights that had plowed into us, then left us for dead in the middle of the Coral Sea. I remembered it as soon as I stepped out of the forest.

A tent was pitched beneath some palm trees, and a small aluminum dinghy had been dragged up onto the beach nearby. But that's not what stopped me in my tracks. Anchored in the middle of the narrow bay was a big blue-and-gray ocean-going launch with *Sharee* painted on its bow. I stared at it for a few seconds. The *Sharee's* three powerful outboard motors and the shape of its flying deck looked strikingly familiar.

Something else looked familiar too.

My brother Nathan has a friend who's a pig hunter, and he has four of the ugliest, meanest dogs you're ever likely to meet. The ugliest and meanest by far is a stocky black, brown and white pit bull terrier called Tyson. I've seen a video of Tyson attacking a wild boar nearly ten times his size, and the poor pig didn't stand a chance.

The dog I saw as I stepped out of the trees was a dead ringer for Tyson. But this one wasn't hunting pigs, it was hunting me.

# 15

# GET RID OF HIM

The pit bull came stalking forward like a squat, boxy-headed tiger. Or like a tiger *shark* that's grown legs. If I'd never met Tyson, I might have stood there and hoped for the best. That's what you're supposed to do if a dog comes at you – stay still, don't make eye contact and, most important of all, don't run away. But I knew Tyson; I'd seen what he could do to a four-hundred-pound wild boar. I turned and ran.

A piercing whistle came from the direction of the tent. A man shouted, "Bruce, get back here!"

It was a chilling coincidence – a dog with a shark's name.

"Bruce!" the man bellowed again.

But Bruce wasn't listening. He was in fight mode. Pit bulls are bred to fight, and Bruce was listening to his instincts, not to the shouting man.

I was listening to *my* instincts too. Or my legs were. But my two legs were no match for Bruce's four. By the time I was twenty yards into the forest, the pit bull had narrowed the distance between us from about a hundred and ten feet to less than seventy-five. I could hear him behind me, his thundering paws, his panting breath, but otherwise he was silent. Dogs that are serious about fighting don't bother with barking; they save their energy for the important stuff: chasing, attacking, killing.

I was running flat out. But the seventy-five feet were down to fifty.

Fortythirtytwentyten ...

*Climb a tree!* my panicked brain was telling me.

Already I'd run past lots, but none that looked suitable to climb – not in a hurry, anyway. I was in a big hurry, but so was Bruce behind me. He was *right* behind me now.

Nineeightsevensixfive ...

I hurtled out into the open. I was in a clearing. Directly ahead of me, on the other side of the clearing, was a heavy thicket covered with fishing net. I charged towards it. I didn't pause to wonder about the net; I simply flung myself at the thicket, jumping as I did so. *Clang!* I hit something solid that rattled like iron, and there was a huge commotion of flapping wings, but all that concerned me was getting away from the pit bull. My fingers grabbed hold and up I went. *Snap!* went Bruce's jaws, spraying a mist of warm saliva on my bare heels as I swung my feet up and away. There was a yowl of frustration when the dog realized I'd escaped.

I found myself on a wobbly, six-foot-high platform. It wasn't a thicket at all, but a man-made structure of iron mesh covered with fishing net and palm fronds and snapped branches. There were dozens of birds below me, and they seemed to be trapped. They fluttered around in panic as I crawled across the creaking iron mesh above them. Slowly, my mind put the details together.

Netting + mesh + trapped birds = *birdcage!*

I was on top of a birdcage. A whole pile of them, in fact. The cages were stacked three or four high and lined up in a row about six feet wide and thirty feet long.

It didn't make sense. Why would anyone keep caged birds on a deserted island sixty miles from the Australian mainland? And why would they hide them under fishing nets and leafy branches?

There wasn't time to puzzle over it. A bald man wearing just a pair of shorts and flip-flops came pounding up through the trees from the same direction I had come. When he saw me, his face turned as mean as Bruce's.

"Get down from there!" he roared.

"But the dog ..."

The bald man grabbed Bruce roughly by the collar and dragged him back from the cages. "Climb down slowly," he said to me. "Don't scare the birds."

I tried my best, but the frightened birds went crashing around in their cages like big, brightly-colored pinballs. Most of them were parrots. Down at the far end was a single large cage containing something much bigger than a parrot. I couldn't see through all the mesh and branches, but whatever was in there was going off – slamming into the sides of its cage with such force that the whole structure rattled and clanged and shook.

"Are they wild or something?" I asked, when I

reached the ground.

"Shut up and get away from the cages!" Baldy snapped. "And don't try to run away, or I'll set the dog on you."

Why would I run away? Baldy seemed really mad at me for upsetting the birds, but I wasn't *scared* of him. I was scared of Bruce, though. His nasty yellow eyes were fixed hungrily on me, and his whole body quivered with the excitement of the hunt.

"Where did you come from?" Baldy asked.

"I got washed off the reef on Utopia Island."

He gave me a disbelieving look. "You swam all the way here?"

"Kind of," I said. I thought about telling him the story I'd been rehearsing, but decided not to. Something very weird was going on here. "There was a current – it carried me along."

"So no one's with you?"

"No, there's just me," I lied. I didn't want to get Michi mixed up in this – whatever *this* was. "I'm sorry for scaring your birds."

Most of them had settled down, but not the big thing in the end cage. It was making a horrible grunting sound now, like a wild pig or a gorilla, and it was still trying to bash its way out.

"Who's this?" a voice behind me asked.

A second man came pushing through the shrubs and trees from the direction of the bay. He was dressed like Steve Irwin and wore a leather hat with the brim turned down at the front.

"He reckons he got swept off the other island," Baldy said.

Leather-hat had a piece of cloth tied around his face, like a bank robber in an old cowboy movie. Only his eyes were visible, and they swung in my direction.

"Where's your mate?" he asked.

How did he know about Michi? He must have seen us, I realized, when their launch nearly ran us down last night.

I lied again. "He drowned."

Leather-hat studied me for a moment. His eyes were icy blue, and they seemed to bore right into me. "That's too bad," he said finally.

He turned to Baldy. "Get rid of him."

# 16

# DORIS

I stood there in shock. It was like a very bad dream. Did *getting rid of me* mean what I thought it did?

"We're not murderers," Baldy said. He had to speak loudly because of all the noise coming from the end cage.

"Have you got a better suggestion?" asked Leather-hat. "He's seen the birds. He's seen your face. He could blow our whole operation."

The bald man shrugged. "With the money we made from the last couple of consignments, plus what we're getting tonight, we could be sitting pretty for quite a few years."

"They'd track us down."

"He doesn't know who we are," Baldy said.

"He's seen your face," the masked man reminded him. "He's probably seen the boat as well."

"What boat?" I asked, acting dumb.

They both looked at me. Bruce tugged against Baldy's restraining hand, growling at me and baring his teeth.

"What's your name?" Leather-hat asked.

"Sam Fox."

"Fox, eh?" The corners of his eyes crinkled with amusement. "Then I guess you won't mind sharing a cage with Doris."

It must have been a joke, because he and Baldy started laughing.

"Who's Doris?" I asked.

"A great big chicken," Leather-hat said, with a smirk in his voice.

I felt relieved. They were going to lock me in one of the birdcages rather than get rid of me. I didn't care who or what Doris was. Obviously she wasn't a chicken, otherwise why would they be laughing? But she had to be a bird of some kind, and I wasn't scared of birds.

Until I met Doris.

She was the creature in the end cage. The one kicking up such a ruckus that it was hard to hear what people were saying. She stopped attacking the wire and retreated into the far corner of her tall, narrow cage when Leather-hat lifted the netting to unlock the door.

"Meet your new cell mate," he said.

Doris was huge. She took up half the cage. She was so big she couldn't stand up straight, and her cage was nearly six feet high. She glowered at us through the wire with such a mean look that even Bruce backed away a little.

"You can't put me in there!" I said.

"Would you rather play chasey with the dog?" Leather-hat asked.

I looked at Bruce. I looked at Doris. It was almost too close to call. "Open the door," I said hoarsely.

I edged into the cage and heard the padlock click closed behind me. I was terrified. Cassowaries are the world's most dangerous birds. They look like a cross between an emu and a giant turkey, with a narrow, bony horn on top of their naked blue heads, and huge clawed feet. There are three claws on each foot, but the center one is the most dangerous. Known as the dagger claw, it's as long as a butcher's knife and has three razor-sharp edges. One kick and you're slit open from your chest to your bellybutton. People have been killed by them.

"You two get to know each other," Leather-hat said, dropping the fishing net back into place over the cage door.

I wanted to ask how long they were going to leave me there, but I was too scared to speak in case it antagonized the cassowary. With my back pressed to the wire, I listened to the two men walk away. It was just Doris and me now, standing beak-to-nose in a cage that was barely big enough for both of us.

You aren't meant to make eye contact with savage dogs, and I wondered if it was the same with cassowaries. I carefully lowered my eyes until I was staring at the giant bird's feet. Or, to be specific, at the two wicked-looking dagger claws.

*One false move*, I thought, *and I'll lose my guts*. Literally.

# 17

# LADIES FIRST

I don't know how long Doris and I stood like that.
Maybe it was only five or ten minutes. Maybe it was
half an hour. I was dead on my feet – dead tired, that
is. I had hardly slept in twenty-four hours, and I'd been
swimming or treading water for most of the night. But
I was too scared to move. Every so often, Doris fluffed
her wispy black feathers and made a rumbling noise
deep in her wrinkly blue neck, otherwise she didn't
move either. There was barely *room* to move. We were
squashed into opposite corners of the cage, with only
seven or eight inches separating us. All I could do was
stand there. And think.

Even thinking was difficult. I'd had so little sleep

that my brain wasn't functioning right. But slowly, everything began to make sense.

Baldy and Leather-hat were smugglers. They caught wild birds on the Australian mainland and brought them out to Cowrie Island under cover of darkness in the *Sharee* – the same launch that had nearly run Michi and me down. Then someone in another boat came to collect the birds from the island and take them overseas. The other boat must be big – a large yacht or a converted fishing trawler – because there were a lot of birds. More than would fit on the *Sharee*. Leather-hat must have made several overnight trips from the mainland, while Baldy camped on the island to take care of the birds.

It was obviously a big operation. A lot of money was involved. According to my brother, collectors in some countries paid as much as twenty thousand dollars for a single Australian cockatoo. I wondered how much they would pay for a cassowary. The whole consignment must have been worth hundreds of thousands of dollars. No wonder Leather-hat and Baldy had been so annoyed when I showed up. No wonder they wanted to get rid of me. They were probably hoping Doris would do the job for them.

But so far the cassowary hadn't done anything. Both of us stood there, waiting for the other to make the first move.

It was Doris's drinking water that finally broke our stalemate. Her rectangular plastic water dish was hooked to the wire mesh down near my feet. Even after all Doris's banging and crashing earlier, there was still some water in it. Looking at the water, I realized how thirsty I was. I was parched. But I was too scared to move. Doris fluffed her feathers again, and this time I couldn't help myself – I raised my eyes. And saw that Doris was looking down at the water just as intently as I had been.

Then it dawned on me – the cassowary wanted a drink as badly as I did, but like me, she was too scared to move.

"Would you like some water, Doris?" I asked softly.

Very slowly, moving just an inch at a time, I bent my knees and slid my back down the wire until I was sitting on the cage floor. Doris towered over me, blocking out half the daylight. Her legs looked like tree trunks. Her feet, with those two terrible dagger claws, were like the feet of some long-extinct dinosaur bird. One kick, and I'd be extinct too. *Don't make any sudden moves*, I cautioned myself. Doris glared as I reached slowly for the water dish.

This was the critical moment. I was crouching directly in front of the cassowary's dagger claws. If she thought I was stealing her water, she might let fly with a kick to my head. A drop of sweat rolled into one of my eyes as I carefully unhooked the dish from the wire. Above me, Doris made a low, booming sound deep in her neck – it sounded like a warning – but her feet stayed put. With shaking hands, I lifted the water dish slowly past my mouth (Torture! I was *dying* for a sip!), past my nose, past my eyes and offered it to the cassowary standing over me.

"Here, Doris," I said softly. My mouth was so dry I could hardly talk. "Ladies first."

The huge bird didn't move. She towered over me, threatening, watchful, suspicious. Not just my hands, but my arms and upper body were shaking now – so badly that I was worried I was going to spill the water. But I was more worried about Doris attacking me. With both my hands above my head, I was offering her a wide-open target. A free kick. And if she kicked, I had no chance. It would all be over in a second.

"I'm your friend, Doris," I whispered.

She blinked. Slowly, she lowered her big blue head towards the water dish. Then stopped halfway. I held my breath. My whole body trembled with a combination of fear and exhaustion. If I had to wait much longer, I was going to pass out. A fly buzzed around my face, and I closed my eyes. The moment they were closed, I felt a gentle vibration through the plastic sides of the water dish. I opened my eyes. Doris was drinking!

"You two get to know each other," Leather-hat had said, when he locked me in with the big, wild cassowary. But he'd been joking. He thought Doris wouldn't let anyone get to know her at such close quarters. Now she was drinking out of my hands. But I wanted her to stop. I didn't want her to drink *all* the water.

*Please leave some for me!* I begged her, in my mind.

I got my wish. Doris lifted her head and looked down at me over the rim of the dish. *Your turn*, she seemed to be saying. There was about an inch left. The water was cloudy with dirt and grit and bits of floating leaves and twigs and even an ant or two, but I drank it down to the very last drop.

It was the most delicious drink I'd ever tasted.

# 18

# TUG-OF-WAR

"Wakey, wakey!" a man's voice said.

I blinked my eyes open, surprised to find myself curled up in a corner of the cage. And even more surprised to find Doris sitting on the floor beside me. We both scrambled to our feet when Baldy lifted a section of camouflaged fishing net clear of the wire mesh, and Bruce the pit bull pressed his ugly nose against it.

"What's going on?" I asked, still half-asleep.

"It's feeding time," Baldy said. He was wearing a khaki shirt and carried two green plastic buckets filled with seeds and chopped fruit. "Care for some lunch?"

I was ravenously hungry, but I didn't feel like eating bird food. A glance at my watch told me it was

1:15. I'd been locked in the cage for nearly five hours. "How much longer are you going to keep me here?"

"We'll let you out tonight," Baldy said. "When we leave."

I watched him shuffling through a big bunch of keys. He and Leather-hat would have to take me out of Doris's cage when the boat from overseas came to pick up the birds. But what would they do with me then?

"Let me out now," I said. "I'll go over to the other side of the island, and I won't bother you again."

"It's more complicated than that," Baldy said, unlocking one of the small cages further along. It contained two scared-looking red-and-green parrots. "There are planes and boats out looking for you."

"I'll stay out of sight until tomorrow."

"We can't take that risk," he said.

I was thinking fast. Baldy was my only hope. I knew what Leather-hat wanted to do with me. "If they ever catch up with you, I'll speak in your defense," I promised. "I'll tell them you let me go, and the judge will give you a lighter sentence."

Baldy filled a metal bowl and placed it in with the two frightened parrots. "Nobody's going to catch me," he said.

"I'll tell them how the other man wanted to kill me, but you wouldn't let him."

"Nobody wants to kill anybody," Baldy said, going to the next cage.

There was a movement in the trees behind him, and I nearly let out a gasp of surprise when Michi came staggering into the clearing. He stopped when he saw me. His jaw dropped slowly open. It must have really confused him to see me in a birdcage. My eyes darted to Baldy, who had his back to the trees as he carefully inserted a key into another padlock. Then I glanced at Bruce, still sitting outside Doris's and my cage with his cruel yellow eyes fixed on me.

"Kidnapping is a *very bad* crime," I said loudly, catching Michi's eye and trying to wave him back into the trees without Baldy noticing. "*Very, very bad!*" I said, even louder.

Baldy frowned at me. "Keep your voice down."

Michi was frowning at me too. He opened his mouth to speak.

"*Very bad!*" I cried, drowning him out.

All along the line of cages, the semi-wild parrots began flapping and squawking and hurling themselves against the wire. But Michi just stood there with his mouth open.

"*Very, very, very bad!*" I shouted, desperate to get my message across.

"Stop the racket!" snarled Baldy. "You're scaring the birds."

I wanted to stop. Doris was getting scared too. If she panicked like the other birds, I'd be history. But I had to warn Michi to get out of sight before either the smuggler or his dog turned around and saw him. Bruce would tear him to shreds.

Suddenly, I had an idea. Pointing at the pit bull, I lowered my voice and said, "*Bad* Bruce."

Bruce was a name that Michi understood. To him it meant shark, and shark meant danger. I saw his expression change from confusion to fear. Clamping his mouth firmly shut, he began backing slowly towards the trees.

He'd only gone two paces before he trod on a twig. *Snap!* The sound was barely audible above the squawking and fluttering of the parrots in the other cages, but the pit bull heard it. He whipped his ugly head around. I saw what was about to happen. Michi was ten yards away, and the nearest tree was a further five yards back. He would never reach it in time.

There was only one thing to do. I shot my hand through the wire and grabbed Bruce by the collar. Before the dog could swing around and bite me, I dragged him hard up against the side of the cage. He twisted and snarled and strained against his collar. His teeth clashed against the wire and showered me with saliva. But he couldn't get me as long as I held on.

"What do you think you're doing?" yelled Baldy, pounding back along the line of cages.

He reached in to grab me, but the pit bull was so blinded by rage that it snapped at its master's wrist, slicing his stainless steel watch strap in two. The broken watch fell to the ground, and Baldy leapt back out of the way.

"You've asked for it now, kid!" he raged, his face tomato-red, and his fingers trembling as he fumbled with his big bunch of keys.

I slid my left hand through Bruce's collar to help take the strain. The dog was amazingly strong. I had to lower myself to the cage floor and apply my full weight to the heavy leather collar to stop him pulling free. It was a tug-of-war. I tried not to think about Doris behind me, or about Baldy, who was fitting a key into the padlock. In a few seconds he would get the door open. Then I would have to let go. But until that happened, I was determined to hang on. The longer I kept the killer dog from going after Michi, the more chance Michi had of getting away. Baldy still didn't know he was there.

*Run, Michi!* I thought, straining against Bruce's stretching, creaking collar.

But when I looked past Baldy's legs, I got a nasty shock. Michi hadn't retreated any further than the edge of the trees. He stooped to pick up a fallen branch. What was he *doing*? He should be running away, not gathering firewood! I watched, dumbfounded, as Michi began breaking twigs and smaller branches off the main branch. He came to a big one and bent it back and forth, back and forth.

*Don't break it!* I thought, wishing I could somehow project my thoughts – in Japanese – into Michi's head. *Baldy will hear ...*

Too late. The branch broke with a snap.

Baldy looked around and saw Michi. "What the–?" he said.

"Michi, *run!*" I yelled.

# 19

# DAVID AND GOLIATH

Michi didn't run. He calmly broke two more twigs off the branch. Then he hefted it in two hands and turned to face Baldy. He was crazy. What chance did a puny ten-year-old have against a full-grown man?

Baldy must have been thinking the same thing. "Give me the stick, kid," he commanded, walking towards Michi with his hand outstretched.

"He doesn't understand English," I said.

Baldy glanced over his shoulder. "Tell him to drop the stick."

I tried to catch Michi's eye, but the Japanese boy was staring intently at Baldy, watching his every move. What could I say to warn him not to try anything stupid? Baldy was twice his size. He could snap Michi's stick like a twig. He could probably snap *Michi* like a twig.

"Very bad," I said. "Run!"

Michi gave no indication that he'd heard me. Instead of running away from the smuggler, he bent at the waist and solemnly bowed to him.

What did he think he was *doing*?

I soon found out. And so did Baldy.

In the time it takes for a normal person to blink, Michi darted forward and tripped the smuggler with his stick. Baldy landed flat on his backside on the leafy ground. "Oof!" he grunted, as the wind was knocked out of him.

When he saw what happened to his master, Bruce let out a fearsome growl and nearly wrenched his collar out of my sweaty hands. But I held on.

The smuggler was back on his feet. "I don't know how you did that," he said, advancing on Michi with his fists clenched. "But you're going to be sorry."

Michi backed away from him, his stick held at the ready. He looked tiny compared to the smuggler. Even with the stick, he didn't have a chance. I wanted to help him, but all I could do was hang on to Bruce and watch.

Bruce was watching too. And straining at his collar so hard that my fingers were going numb. But I had to hold on. If the pit bull got free now, Michi was dead.

He was probably dead anyway, if the look on Baldy's face was anything to go by. The smuggler's eyes were narrowed. Veins stood out on his temples. His jaw was clenched. Suddenly, he lunged. He moved fast for someone his size. But not fast enough. Michi skipped nimbly to one side, twirled his stick like a juggler, and Baldy crashed to the ground in a big cloud of dust.

Bruce went totally berserk at the sight of his master falling a second time. He nearly pulled my arms out of their sockets. But he could have saved his energy. No way was I letting him go.

The smuggler climbed slowly back to his feet. He was breathing heavily. There was dust all over his clothes. He glared at Michi. Small as he was, the Japanese boy was obviously trained in martial arts. Baldy wasn't taking any more chances. Turning, he limped over to the trees on the other side of the clearing and broke off a dead branch. It was longer than Michi's and four times as thick. It looked like an oversized baseball bat. Baldy slapped it twice against his palm. *Thwack, thwack!*

"Okay, kid, let's see how good you are," he muttered.

Slowly, they circled each other. They looked like David and Goliath. It was frightening to watch. Michi might have been quick, but Baldy was much too big, much too strong. There was a cruel, predatory look on the smuggler's face as he advanced on the boy. He meant business. Michi backed away from him, leading him in circles. He held his stick in two hands, like a jujitsu staff, but he wasn't trying to use it. One blow from Baldy's club would smash it to bits. One blow would crack Michi's skull.

All I could do was watch. I was locked in with the cassowary, and my hands were locked around Bruce's collar. There was nothing I could do to help.

Suddenly, Baldy swung his massive club. *Whoosh!* Michi skipped backwards. It passed within an inch of his chest. Baldy came at him again. This time Michi jumped straight up, like a kangaroo. The huge club swished harmlessly beneath him. Had it connected, it would have shattered both his legs. Michi landed, dainty as a cat in his brown leather shoes, and danced away from Baldy as the angry smuggler swung his club a third time. *Whoosh!* Missed again. Around and around they went, the man lunging, swinging, shouting each time he missed; the boy ducking, jumping, backpedaling, his own stick poised, but never striking. All the time his eyes remained fixed on Baldy's, reading his every move before it happened.

*Whoosh! Whoosh! Whoosh!*

Baldy was growing tired, and his swings were becoming less and less accurate. His chest heaved. His shirt was drenched with sweat. His face was as red as a tomato and distorted with a mixture of rage and frustration. But still he followed Michi, swinging wildly now, barely taking the time to aim. No longer concentrating.

It took Baldy completely by surprise. Michi moved with the speed of a striking taipan. For two minutes he'd been retreating. Suddenly, he attacked. Using his stick like a pole-vaulter, he launched himself high in the air over Baldy's swinging club and lashed out with his right foot. In karate it's called a flying side kick, but in karate there's no staff, so you don't get so much air. And you don't wear shoes in any of the martial arts, but Michi hadn't had time to take his off. Which was bad luck for Baldy. The toe of Michi's heavy leather shoe struck him squarely in the temple. *Whop!* Baldy went down like a sack of wet cement.

I watched Michi pick up Baldy's club and toss it into the trees. He bent to check that the unconscious man was breathing properly, then came walking warily towards the row of cages. He looked doubtfully at Bruce, who was growling at him like a lion and scrabbling his paws in the dirt in a renewed effort to break free of my grip.

"Bad?" he asked, pointing at the angry pit bull with his stick.

"He's called Bruce," I said, "same as the shark."

Michi nodded solemnly. "Very bad!"

"Let him go," a deep voice commanded.

We both looked in the direction of the trees. Leather-hat stood over Baldy's motionless body. He held a diver's spear gun in one hand. The spear's deadly, barbed point was aimed straight at Michi's heart.

# 20

# A MASTER AT WORK

"Let go of the dog," Leather-hat said, "or your Japanese friend gets it."

This time Leather-hat hadn't bothered to cover his face. Which could only mean one thing: He wasn't afraid of us seeing his face because he had no intention of letting us go. Ever.

I glanced at Michi. He had dropped his stick and raised both hands in the air. His face was expressionless, but I could see his eyes darting back and forth, assessing the situation.

"He's only a kid," I said. "The dog will rip him to shreds."

"Most likely," Leather-hat agreed with a smirk.

He glanced down at Baldy, who groaned and rubbed the side of his head. "But from the way he handled Sebastian, I reckon he might put up a bit of a fight."

So Baldy's name was Sebastian. I wondered if I would live long enough to tell the police.

"He doesn't understand English," I said, stalling for time. The spear gun was heavy, designed to be carried underwater, not on land. I could see Leather-hat's hand trembling from the strain of holding it. With every passing second, his aim was growing worse. "He's got no idea who you are, or what's going on with the birds," I said. "Let him go."

Leather-hat shook his head, and the spear wobbled all over the place. "No. *You* let the dog go."

"Make me," I said, deliberately provoking him.

He narrowed his eyes and turned the spear gun in my direction. It was exactly what I wanted him to do.

"On the count of three ..." he said.

But I wasn't waiting for any countdown. "Michi, *run!*" I yelled.

What happened next was almost too quick for the eye to see. Instead of running, Michi rolled forward in a lightning-fast somersault. He gathered his stick off the ground and, while still upside down, flicked it sideways.

I had underestimated Leather-hat. His arm was tired, and I'd thought his aim would be poor. But when he pulled the trigger, the spear was pointed exactly where he wanted it to go. Its stainless-steel shaft flashed across the clearing like a single pulse from a strobe light, coming straight at my chest at roughly one hundred eighty miles per hour.

There was no time to react, no time to get out of the way. There wasn't even time to blink. So I saw exactly what happened.

The spear and Michi's stick collided six feet short of the cage. The stick wasn't heavy enough to deflect the spear by more than a few degrees, but those few degrees were enough to save my life. Instead of burying itself in my chest, the spear's hardened steel tip shot past my left hand, missing Bruce's neck by a hair's breadth. It passed harmlessly beneath my elbow, flew between Doris's legs and out through the back of the cage.

Apart from Michi's stick, the spear touched only one thing on its way through the cage: Bruce's collar. And it sliced it cleanly in two.

One moment I had been straining every muscle

in my body against seventy pounds of angry pit bull terrier, the next moment I was having a tug-of-war with nothing but a broken strip of studded leather. I shot backwards across the floor of the cage and slammed into Doris's bony legs. She collapsed on top of me. For a few seconds, everything went black. I was smothered in a dry waterfall of soft, dark feathers, with a heavy, warm body pressing down on top.

I couldn't breathe.

Then Doris scrambled back to her feet. One of those feet was planted squarely on my chest. She was heavy. The tip of one long, curved dagger claw pressed painfully against my racing heart. With one twist of her foot, the huge bird could have opened my ribcage like an eggshell. But the cassowary wasn't aware she was standing on me. Her full attention was focused on something outside the cage. I raised my head to look.

In the center of a great cloud of dust, Bruce was chasing Michi in circles. Michi wasn't trying to run away – nobody could outrun a charging pit bull – instead, he was concentrating on twirling, jumping and sidestepping.

I was watching a master at work.

Martial arts are as much about defense as attack, and Michi was using all his skill to outwit his four-legged pursuer. He moved like a matador evading an angry bull. Again and again, the dog swerved and attacked, but each time its jaws snapped closed around nothing but empty air. Michi seemed to be everywhere at once – in front of the dog, behind it, above its head. Never had I seen such speed, such fluid movements, such finely honed reactions – except in the movies.

But Michi couldn't keep it up. After fifteen seconds he was tiring, and his reactions were slowing down. Bruce, on the other hand, seemed to be getting faster – his reactions were becoming sharper and quicker. Pit bulls are bred to fight. They are fighting machines, both physically and mentally. Much like a competitor in a karate competition, they size up their opponent quickly and learn their strengths and weaknesses. After twenty seconds, Bruce had learned enough about Michi to anticipate his next move. When Michi leapt in the air to avoid another charge, Bruce suddenly changed his line of attack and leapt as well. Michi saw the dog coming and twisted sideways, but he wasn't quick enough. *Snap!* The pit bull had him by the ankle.

I thought it was all over then, and the dog must have thought so too. But Michi had fooled us both. In the short time that he and Bruce had been engaged in their frantic game of cat and mouse, Michi had led his pursuer slowly towards the edge of the forest. Now they were right underneath the low branch of a big Pisonia tree. When Michi jumped into the air, he grabbed hold with both hands and dragged himself up.

Bruce swung from his ankle like a pendulum.

I wondered how long Michi could hang on. His skinny arms were trembling from supporting both his weight and the dog's. The pit bull looked nearly as big as him. It growled as it hung there. It was only four inches off the ground, but it wasn't going to let go until it pulled Michi down from the branch. And that would be the end of him.

"Help him!" I cried, lying helpless on the floor of the cage with the cassowary's foot on my chest.

Baldy was sitting up halfway across the clearing. There was blood on his ear and a cruel expression on his face as he watched Leather-hat walk towards the tree. Leather-hat prodded Michi in the stomach with the spear gun.

"Get down," he said.

"He can't get down," I shouted. "The dog will kill him."

Leather-hat grinned in my direction. "You're next," he promised.

Then he whacked Michi on the legs with the spear gun. I saw tears gather in Michi's eyes, but still he hung on.

"I *said* get down!" snarled the smuggler. And he drew back the spear gun to hit Michi again.

# 21

# BOY VERSUS PIT BULL

Michi watched me over the top of Leather-hat's head. He saw me raise one foot towards the latch on the cage door. Moving slowly, so as not to alarm the cassowary still standing on my chest, I poked my toes through a gap in the mesh.

I'd just noticed something: Baldy had left the key in the padlock. Capturing it between my first two toes, I pulled the small brass padlock halfway into the cage and slowly twisted my foot sideways. The key jammed against one of the wires. It started turning. *Click!* The padlock popped open and fell to the ground with a clatter. I held my breath in case the smugglers heard it, but neither man looked around.

Leather-hat raised the spear gun to hit Michi a second time.

I had to act quickly. Jamming half my foot through the wire, I shoved the door latch sideways. It made a loud, metallic squeal. Both Leather-hat and Baldy turned startled faces in my direction.

"What the–" growled Leather-hat.

That was all he managed to say. He shouldn't have taken his eyes off Michi. Michi had a dog hanging off one foot, but his other foot was free. And Michi's feet were deadly weapons.

*Thump!*

Leather-hat never knew what hit him. He dropped the spear gun and fell in a heap. His heavy-brimmed hat went spinning off across the clearing like a frisbee.

"Hey, don't do that!" cried Baldy. He lurched to his feet and came staggering towards me.

I kicked the cage door open.

Who knows how long Doris had been locked up, but when she saw a chance to escape, she took it. She bolted from the cage at roughly thirty miles per hour. Baldy saw her coming and spread his arms to shoo her back in.

It was brave of him, but stupid.

Doris had a sniff of freedom in her nostrils, and she wasn't going to stop for anything. Baldy had no chance. I almost felt sorry for him. Almost. The cassowary lowered her head and plowed into him, horn first, like a charging rhinoceros. *Whomp*! Right in the stomach.

When the dust cleared, Baldy lay flat on his back beside Leather-hat. The only sign of Doris was a long black feather that fluttered silently to the ground on the other side of the clearing. And the sound of her heavy feet thumping down the slope towards the bay.

I staggered out of the cage. There was no time to lose. Both smugglers would be out of action for a while, but Michi's and my troubles were far from over. Michi still dangled from the branch with the pit bull swinging from his ankle. He tried kicking it with his other foot, but he couldn't reach. Weird. I had to look twice before I understood what was happening. The pit bull's jaws were locked onto Michi's sock, not his ankle, and the sock was stretching. A long loop of it hung out of his tightly-laced shoe. The sock might rip at any moment. Or Michi might let go. Then the pit bull would make mincemeat of him.

I raced around behind the cage and found the

spear embedded in a tree trunk. It took a moment to wriggle it free, then I ran back for the spear gun. I didn't want to hurt the dog, but it was either him or us. Kneeling between the two unconscious smugglers, I tried desperately to load the gun. But I couldn't figure out how to do it. *Hurry, hurry!* I thought, in a panic. My hands were shaking so badly I dropped the spear.

"Sam, *tyuui site!*"

I looked up just in time to see Michi's shoe slip from his foot, dragged off by the weight of the pit bull. Bruce crashed to the ground. He was up in a split second. He snarled at Michi dangling from the tree above him. Then he turned his ugly head in my direction.

*Uh oh!*

When the pit bull bared his teeth at me, they looked every bit as fearsome as a tiger shark's. For a moment, the dog seemed to smile.

Then he charged.

There wasn't time to pick up the spear. I used the gun to fend him off. Or tried to. Quick as a sprung rat trap, the pit bull chomped the metal shaft in its teeth and wrenched the useless weapon from my grip.

I began backing slowly away. Out of the corner of my eye, I saw Michi drop to the ground, stagger slightly, then limp off into the trees. I was on my own. It was just me and Bruce now. Boy versus pit bull.

Bruce dropped the spear gun and came stalking after me, like a cat playing with an injured mouse. I wasn't injured, but I felt as helpless as a mouse. My karate training had helped when I was fighting the tiger shark, but facing a pit bull I was hopelessly outclassed. All I could do was try to get away. I shuffled slowly backwards. The cages were behind me. If I could just reach them, I might have a chance.

But I wasn't looking where I was going. My heels bumped into something, and I lost my balance. As I tumbled slowly backwards over Baldy's lifeless body, I glimpsed Michi racing up behind the pit bull, a large stick raised above his head like a samurai sword. But he wasn't going to make it. Bruce would be on me before Michi reached us.

Even as I hit the ground, I was rolling sideways in a last ditch attempt to evade the attacking pit bull.

The attack never came. Instead, I heard a pounding sound, like horses' hooves. The ground trembled. A huge black shape shot straight over me.

For a nanosecond it blocked out the sun. Then, with a rush of wind, it was gone.

I sat up in time to see Doris galloping off into the trees, with Bruce hot on her heels.

Michi helped me to my feet. He grinned and pointed with Baldy's stick into the forest where the cassowary and pit bull had just disappeared.

"Roadrunner!" he said. Obviously Michi watched cartoons in English too.

"Cassowary," I told him. I didn't know why she'd come back, but Doris had saved our bacon by leading Bruce away.

"Let's go," I said, and led Michi off in the other direction.

# 22

# CRAZY KID!

When we emerged from the forest behind the smugglers' tent, we discovered why Doris had come charging back through the clearing. Help had arrived. Help for Michi and me, that is. Not for Doris. One look at the Zodiac inflatable boat puttering up the narrow bay towards her, and she must have freaked out and doubled back the way she had come.

Three men were on board. They must have come from a larger vessel waiting out in deeper water. From their clothing, I knew they weren't policemen or naval officers. Perhaps they were from the Volunteer Coast Guard. They steered their craft around the anchored *Sharee* and nudged it ashore beside Baldy and Leather-hat's dinghy. The outboard motor fell silent.

"G'day," I said, leading Michi down to meet them. "It's sure good to see you."

The men stepped out of the Zodiac and pulled its broad triangular bow up onto the sand. One of them was tall and wore a blue jacket and captain's hat.

"Who are you?" he asked. He had a strange accent.

"Sam Fox," I said. "And this is Michi. We're the ones you're looking for."

The captain seemed puzzled. He spoke to one of the other men in a language I didn't recognize. The other man shrugged and replied in the same language. As they talked, I noticed a bulge beneath the captain's jacket, just below his left armpit. It looked scarily like a pistol. He turned back to Michi and me, his brow creased in a frown as he studied our tattered and filthy clothes.

"This is a surprise," he said. "We expected to meet Charlie Willis and Sebastian Crowe, not a pair of boys."

Suddenly, the penny dropped. These men weren't looking for us; they were looking for Leather-hat and Baldy. They were the overseas buyers, coming to pick up the birds!

"They're up with the consignment," I said quickly.

"I'm Sebastian's nephew, and this is my friend Michi."

The captain nibbled his lower lip. He didn't seem totally convinced. "Where is the, er, consignment?"

"Just through there." I pointed into the forest.

"Show us," he said.

*No way,* I thought. As soon as they found Sebastian and Charlie (alias Baldy and Leather-hat), our number would be up. "It's only fifty yards," I said. "You can hear the birds from here."

It was true. The caged parrots were chattering and squawking like budgies in an aviary. The captain listened for a moment, then nodded.

"Jimmy, you come with me," he ordered one of the men. "Rollo, stay here and keep the children company."

The captain was right not to trust me, but I resented it all the same. And I resented being called a child.

He would soon learn how badly he'd underestimated us.

I watched the two men disappear into the forest. The third man, Rollo, leaned against a palm tree and lit a cigarette. He wore jeans and a T-shirt. There was no bulge of a gun, but he had a large bowie knife in a sheath on his belt. I caught Michi's eye. Did he have any idea what was going on? We had sixty seconds, maximum, before the other two reached the clearing. Then the bird poop would hit the fan.

"Where are you going?" Rollo asked me.

"I need a drink," I said, walking casually towards the tent.

Michi followed me, right on cue.

So did Rollo.

All three of us crowded into the tent. There wasn't much room. A low folding bed and a sleeping bag took up much of the floor space. It confirmed my theory that Baldy had camped on the island while Leather-hat ferried the birds over from the mainland. Judging by the mess, I guessed Baldy had been there for several nights.

A big cooler sat next to the center pole. I lifted the lid. I'd had nothing to eat for twenty-four hours, and my mouth watered at the sight of all the food – bread, cheese, hot dogs, corned beef – but there wasn't time to eat. I picked up a carton of eggs and tossed it to Rollo.

"Catch!"

Instinctively, he caught it. Before he had time to register surprise, I shoved him hard in the chest. Still holding the eggs, Rollo took half a step backwards, tripped on a pile of clothes and sat down so heavily on the flimsy bed that it gave way beneath him. Even before he hit the floor, I was backing out of the tent, pushing Michi behind me with one hand and reaching for the center pole with the other.

The tent collapsed in a big, squirming heap. It was squirming because Rollo was caught somewhere inside it. I tossed the tent pole aside and beckoned to Michi.

"Quick, we'll take one of the boats!"

I had forgotten – again – that Michi didn't understand English. Instead of following me, he stooped and picked up the tent pole.

*Crazy kid! What did he think … ?*

That thought never got finished. Because suddenly, I saw why Michi needed the tent pole. I skidded to a halt.

*Shishkebab!*

Halfway between us and the two boats stood Bruce the pit bull.

# SITTING DUCKS

I hardly recognized him. The dog's head was hanging, he was covered in bleeding scratches, and one paw was raised painfully off the ground.

It was obvious what had happened. Pit bulls are bred to fight other pit bulls, not cassowaries. Doris had given him a lesson in jungle combat.

When Michi waved the tent pole, Bruce whimpered like a frightened puppy and scuttled out of our way.

We ran for the boats. I could hear angry voices coming from the direction of the birdcages. Behind us, Rollo was using his knife to hack his way out of the collapsed tent.

Michi ran to the nearest boat, Leather-hat and Baldy's aluminum dinghy, but I grabbed his arm.

"Not that one," I said. "The other one's got a motor."

We pushed the Zodiac out into the water and scrambled over its squashy rubber sides. I could hear shouting in the forest behind us. Further along the shoreline, Rollo was clambering out of the pile of twisted canvas that was no longer recognizable as a tent. His clothes were splattered with eggs. I tried not to watch him as I struggled with the Zodiac's outboard motor. It had a rope starter like a lawn mower. I yanked on it. One pull, two pulls, three pulls. Rollo came tearing along the beach. I could hear voices in the trees, growing louder every second. Four pulls. Michi was using his hands like paddles, but we were still only a few yards from shore and going backwards. Five pulls.

*Is the fuel turned on?* I thought suddenly.

I found a twist valve on the rubber hose leading from the fuel tank and turned it.

Six pulls. The engine roared into life, and the boat shot forward. But it was facing the shore. We met Rollo head-on as he came splashing out towards us. The Zodiac plowed into him, toppling him over backwards. He disappeared under the front of the boat, his fingers clutching at the slippery fabric. I swung the engine sideways, and the Zodiac began a slow U-turn. It rocked from side to side, as Rollo fought to hold on. Only his hands and forearms were visible, clinging to the bow.

"Michi, try to make him let go!" I cried.

Even though he couldn't understand my words, Michi knew what I meant. He nodded and scrabbled towards the front of the boat.

I looked over my shoulder. The smuggler named Jimmy came running out of the trees. The captain wouldn't be far behind, and he had a gun. As Jimmy charged down the beach, I twisted the throttle grip as far as it would go. With a roar, we shot out into the bay. Michi lost his balance and fell back against my legs. I risked another look back and saw the captain appear at the edge of the forest. He and Leather-hat were supporting Baldy, who limped between them. When the captain saw what was going on, he let go of Baldy and whipped out his pistol. He raised it as he ran to the water's edge. We were only twenty-five feet from shore. Sitting ducks.

"Look out!" I yelled, pushing Michi down.

I would have liked to join him in the bottom of the boat, but I had to steer. I crouched behind the outboard motor. There was a deafening bang as a bullet crashed into the transom that supported it. Wood splinters showered all over us. A second bullet ricocheted off the engine housing. In a desperate effort to present a more difficult target, I set us on a zigzag course towards the mouth of the bay. Another bullet buzzed overhead, missing me by inches.

Then the shooting stopped. I soon saw the reason. Rollo's head had appeared over the bow. He had grabbed hold of one of the stainless-steel towing rings and hauled himself up. The captain had to stop shooting for fear of hitting him.

"Take the engine," I said to Michi, motioning with my hand.

He seemed to understand. We swapped places. I crawled towards the front of the Zodiac. Towards Rollo. He had hold of two towing rings now and was halfway in. I reached for one of his hands and twisted the fingers back, forcing him to let go. The smuggler cursed me and slid down, almost out of view. I tried the same thing on his other hand, but he closed it in a tight fist. He was strong. Even with two hands, I was finding it hard to make him let go.

"*Tyuui site!*" yelled Michi.

Instinctively, I made an upward elbow block. And not a moment too soon. While I'd been struggling with Rollo's left hand, his right hand had drawn the bowie knife from its sheath and swung it up over the edge of the Zodiac in a deadly arc. I blocked it right above my head. Its big, serrated blade flashed in the sunlight. For several seconds we had a silent wrestling match. Rollo was pushing down, and I was pushing up. He was bigger and stronger than me, but I had the advantage of being inside the boat. I wedged my legs against its tight, air-filled sides and used my whole body as a lever. Slowly, the knife wavered and began to lift.

Then we hit a wave. The Zodiac's bow reared up, and the smuggler was thrown off balance. For a split second, he stopped pushing against my arm as he adjusted his grip on the towing ring. It was all the time I needed. I formed a karate ridge-hand and struck him with all my strength right on the point of his elbow. It hurt my hand, but it hurt Rollo more. He screamed, dropped the knife, and slid from view.

"Karate, okay!" Michi said, smiling at me from the other end of the Zodiac as we rocked across another wave.

I peered cautiously over the side. We were clear of the bay and moving out into open water. A big ocean cruiser lay at anchor just beyond the breakers. The overseas smugglers' boat. For a moment I considered telling Michi to steer towards it, then changed my mind. I didn't even know how to pull up an anchor, much less operate such a large craft. The Zodiac was our best chance of escaping. I looked back. Rollo's head bobbed in the surf. He yelled at me and made an aggressive gesture above the waves with one hand. I couldn't hear him over the roar of the outboard's motor, but I could guess what was on his mind. He was a bad loser.

Five hundred feet behind him, slowly crossing the bay towards the *Sharee*, was a small row boat with four men on board.

Michi and I had won this round, but I had a very bad feeling about the next one.

# 24

# THE FINAL ROUND

The Zodiac was no match for Leather-hat's powerful launch. We had a five-minute head start, but by the time we rounded the end of Cowrie Island, the *Sharee* was only a few hundred yards behind us. And gaining fast.

Michi held the throttle wide-open. I pointed at a line of trees poking above the horizon. Utopia Island. He nodded and adjusted our course slightly, until we were heading straight for it. But his face remained grim, and I suspect mine was the same. Both of us knew we weren't going to make it.

Then Michi's expression changed. His eyes lit up with excitement. "*Soko ni booto ga arimasu!*" he said, pointing.

I twisted around to look. Another boat! It had just appeared around the end of Utopia Island. But could they see us? I glanced back at the smugglers' launch. It was only a hundred and fifty yards away now. Close enough for me to identify the two figures on the flying bridge. Leather-hat was at the helm. The captain stood beside him, gripping the canvas sun canopy for support and holding a small, dark object in his other hand. Even at that distance, I saw what it was.

I turned my back on the smugglers. Bracing my legs against the Zodiac's sides, I stood up and waved my hands above my head. But it was hopeless. The other boat was nearly half a mile away. They would never see me. The Zodiac bounced over a swell, and I had to drop to my knees with a thump to avoid being bounced overboard. Then I noticed a gap in the floor. The bottom of the Zodiac was lined with marine plywood floor plates, and two had come loose when I landed. There was something underneath. A box of some kind, with red writing on it. Only one word was visible through the gap in the floor plates. Or part of a word: MERGENCY. I lifted one of the panels. In the small compartment underneath were two life jackets and a black waterproof case with the following inscription:

## MARINE SIGNAL FLARE
## USE ONLY IN EMERGENCY

This *was* an emergency. I dragged the case out and opened it. Inside was the biggest pistol I'd ever seen. Its barrel wasn't particularly long, but it was as wide as a truck's exhaust pipe. Packed next to it were two shells. They resembled shotgun shells, except they were much larger – almost as big as a tin can. The flare pistol broke open exactly like my brother's twelve-gauge shotgun. I slid one of the shells into the breech and snapped it closed. I cocked the hammer, then raised the oversized pistol above my head.

Michi watched me, his teeth clenched, his short, spiky hair ruffling in the wind. Behind him, the *Sharee* rode its churning bow-wave straight towards us. It was fifty yards away and traveling at twice our speed. Leather-hat was going to run us down.

I pulled the trigger.

*Boom!*

The recoil rocked the Zodiac. It nearly blew the pistol out of my hand. A long white smoke trail arced up into the sky. At a height of several hundred feet, the flare exploded in a brilliant red flash. It was too bright to look at, and for a moment, I was partially blinded.

A loud *crack* brought me back to my senses. I threw myself to the bottom of the Zodiac as a bullet whistled overhead. Michi swung the Zodiac sideways. The little outboard motor screamed as he twisted the throttle as far as it would go, but the deep thrum of the launch's engines continued growing louder. Another pistol shot rang out. Michi yelled something in Japanese, but I had no idea what it was. I was lying on something hard. Rolling sideways, I discovered the second flare wedged between two loose floor panels beneath me. With fumbling fingers, I tried to load it into the pistol. A flare gun isn't a weapon, but I figured it could do a lot of damage at close quarters. And the *Sharee* was close. It was right behind us, looming above Michi's head. So close in fact, that I could see the cruel grin on Leather-hat's face as he steered the careening launch on a course that would cut the Zodiac cleanly in two.

Unless we got out of the way first.

"*Turn!*" I screamed at Michi, motioning frantically with my hands.

He shook his head and pointed at the outboard motor. *Shishkebab!* There was a small hole in the engine housing near Michi's finger. A fine spray of gas came spilling out. One of the captain's bullets must have severed the fuel line. We were dead in the water.

And we'd be *totally* dead in about two seconds.

The launch's bow came slicing down on us.

"Jump!" I yelled.

Michi looked terrified. He hesitated for a nanosecond, then hurled himself over the side of the Zodiac. I jumped the other way. The *Sharee* went plowing between us in a whirl of white water, just as it had the night before. But this time I'd been able to jump far enough to one side to avoid making contact with the hull. Its churning bow-wave spun me around a couple of times as the *Sharee* raced past, then I found myself bobbing in the open sea. I had swallowed a bit of water, otherwise I felt okay.

"Sam!" called a desperate, high-pitched voice.

I kicked myself in a half-circle. Michi was four yards away, bobbing up and down in the water, taking big gulps of air every time his mouth was clear. *He's hurt!* was my first panicked thought. Then I remembered that Michi couldn't swim. That's why he had hesitated before jumping out of the Zodiac. But he wasn't panicking; he was only taking breaths when his mouth was above water. I kicked my way over to him.

"It's okay, Michi," I said, trying to sound calm as I swam around behind him. "No, don't grab hold of me, just relax."

He seemed to understand what I was saying and allowed me to support him from behind. As long as he didn't panic, we could stay afloat until the rescue boat arrived. They must have seen my flare.

But I was getting way ahead of myself. We weren't safe yet. Far from it, in fact. Two hundred feet away, another boat rocked gently on the pitching, green-blue sea. Leather-hat stood on the *Sharee's* flying deck, looking through a pair of binoculars. The sun flashed on the twin lenses as they came to rest on Michi and me. Leather-hat passed the binoculars to the captain, then turned to the helm. The three big outboards burbled into life.

"Very bad!" Michi said softly.

His English was better than my Japanese. And unfortunately, he was right. Things looked very bad indeed.

Slowly, the big blue-and-gray launch came around in the water. Michi stiffened in my arms and muttered something I didn't understand. But my eyes told me what my ears didn't. Wrapped around the *Sharee's* bow, like a folded mattress, was the wreck of the Zodiac. Its little outboard motor had flipped over in the collision, and now it dangled upside down above the rest of the wreckage. One of its propeller blades was buried deep in the *Sharee's* hull, holding the crumpled Zodiac in place. Obviously the smugglers didn't know it was there. Leather-hat gunned the throttle, and the funny-looking combination of ocean launch and inflatable boat came churning towards us.

It might have looked funny, but neither Michi nor I were laughing. Our situation was dire. All five smugglers were crowded onto the flying deck now. Leather-hat had the helm, while the other four seemed to be engaged in an argument. Baldy was pointing to starboard and yelling in Leather-hat's ear. Rollo and Jimmy were having a tug-of-war with the binoculars. But it was the captain who I was watching most closely. He was yelling at Leather-hat too, but at the same time he was reloading his pistol.

And that reminded me …

Supporting Michi with one arm, I lifted the flare gun clear of the water. Self-preservation had caused me to hold on to it as I jumped overboard, then I'd shoved it into the band of my shorts when I went to rescue Michi. I wasn't even sure if I'd finished loading it – so much had been going on – but it was our only hope. With a dripping thumb, I pulled the hammer back.

The *Sharee* was fifty yards away and gaining speed. I could see the smugglers' faces clearly now. Baldy was still yelling, but Leather-hat ignored him. His mouth was set in a grim line as he powered the launch towards us like some strange, ocean-going bulldozer, pushing the wrecked Zodiac along beneath its bow in a wave of boiling white foam.

The fifty-yard gap was down to forty yards.

The captain raised his pistol and took aim. So did I. For half a second we eyeballed each other along our pistol barrels. Then – hoping with all my heart that the flare gun was loaded – I lowered my aim and pulled the trigger.

*Boom!*

The recoil pushed Michi and me back in the water and made my ears ring, but it was nothing compared to what followed.

The flare shot low across the water like a smoking tracer shell and slammed into the wreckage of the Zodiac.

Bull's-eye!

I held my breath. The wreckage was wet with the gasoline spraying out of the damaged outboard motor. Any second now ...

*Boom!*

The *Sharee's* bow erupted in a great ball of fire. I dragged Michi under the water as flaming debris fell hissing into the sea all around us. We held our breath for as long as we could, then bobbed back to the surface. Michi was coughing and gasping, but without the hindrance of the flare gun I had two hands to support him, and I held his head clear of the waves.

Twenty-five yards away, the splintered hull of the *Sharee* rolled over like a sounding whale and slid slowly from view. All that remained were five heads bobbing in the water. Baldy was still yelling at Leather-hat (who was minus the hat) and pointing at a big white police launch that came motoring towards us across the wide aquamarine sea.

"Are you satisfied now?" Baldy demanded.

Leather-hat said nothing.

But Michi did. He twisted around in my arms and grinned.

"Sam indestructible!" he said.

# 25

# MICHIKO

Even the police found it hard to believe our story. And Michi couldn't back me up, because he only spoke Japanese. The five smugglers weren't saying anything until they'd spoken to their lawyers. I guess they were too embarrassed to admit that they'd been outwitted by two boys.

In the end, it was Michi's mother who verified my story. She and her husband, along with my parents and the twins, were the first people to greet us when the police delivered us to Utopia Island. Mrs. Takai spoke English and translated what Michi had to say for the amazed police officers.

"That has to be the most incredible story I've

heard in twenty-two years on the force," said Sergeant Thomas, still looking doubtful.

"Michi would not lie," said Mrs. Takai. "Sam Fox is very brave young man."

She bowed to me, and so did her husband and Michi. I bowed back.

"It was nothing," I said modestly.

Mrs. Takai shook her head. "For us is very great thing you do, Sam-san. You saved life of our Michiko."

*Michiko.* Suddenly, the penny dropped, and I realized why Michi had looked familiar. Apart from the short hair, he bore an uncanny resemblance to the world-famous Japanese martial arts actor, Michiko Takai.

*Michiko must be a boy's name too*, I thought. "Your son has the same name as my favorite movie star," I said.

A tiny frown creased Mrs. Takai's brow. "We have no son, Sam-san. Michiko is only child."

This conversation was getting weird. "But Michi's a … a … a … boy!" I stammered.

Mrs. Takai studied me for a moment, frowning. "Michiko had hair cut short for latest movie. She plays boy character. Is good disguise, you think?"

Then she said something in Japanese to Michi and her husband, and both of them smiled.

I stood there feeling foolish. I knew my face was bright red. Michi was a girl! Not only that, but he (I mean *she*) was Michiko Takai – *the* Michiko Takai! Thirteen years old and a genuine black belt. Who'd starred in three blockbuster Japanese martial arts movies. Who did all her own stunts. Whose movie posters were all over my bedroom walls at home ...

I couldn't believe it. I'd spent the last twenty-four hours with the coolest girl on the planet – and all that time, I'd thought she was a boy!

Almost as if she could read my mind, Michi stepped forward, raised herself on tiptoe, and kissed me on the cheek.

Before we separated, she whispered in my ear. "*Anata wa suteki desu, Sam Fox.*"

If I had understood Japanese at the time, my face would have turned even redder than it was already!

# ABOUT THE AUTHOR

Born in New Zealand, Justin D'Ath is one of twelve children. He came to Australia in 1971 to study for the missionary priesthood. After three years, he left the seminary in the dead of night and spent two years roaming Australia on a motorcycle. While doing that he began writing for motorcycle magazines. He published his first novel for adults in 1989. This was followed by numerous award-winning short stories, also for adults. Justin has worked in a sugar mill, on a cattle station, in a mine, on an island, in a laboratory, built cars, picked fruit, driven forklifts and taught writing for twelve years. He wrote his first children's book in 1996. To date he has published twenty-three books. He has two children, two grandchildren, and one dog.

www.justindath.com